GREEN VALLEY JUSTICE

Also by Phillip Underwood
in Thorndike Large Print

Ben Cooper, U.S. Marshal

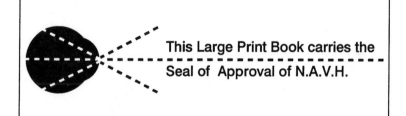

This Large Print Book carries the
Seal of Approval of N.A.V.H.

GREEN VALLEY JUSTICE

Phillip Underwood

Thorndike Press • Thorndike, Maine

Library of Congress Cataloging in Publication Data:

Underwood, Phillip.
    Green Valley justice / Phillip Underwood.
        p. cm.
        ISBN 1-56054-508-9 (alk. paper : lg. print)
    1. Large type books. I. Title.
    [PS3571.N438G7   1992]   92-20218
    813'.54—dc20   CIP

All the characters and events portrayed in this work are
fictitious.

Thorndike Press Large Print edition published in 1992
by arrangement with Walker Publishing Company, Inc.

Cover design by Studio 3.

The tree indicium is a trademark of Thorndike Press.

This book is printed on acid-free, high opacity paper. ∞

To the Memory of
Charles Turner Dixon
1923–90
A milkman with the heart of a gunfighter

PROLOGUE

He was close. Too close for her to make it back to the road and the buggy.

The woods were deep, dark, and still. Only the occasional cry of a faraway hawk broke the intense silence.

Geneva Hendriks looked about at the shadows, searching every tree, every bush. Her fear caused her heart to thump savagely against her ribs.

She took one careful step forward and recoiled as a twig snapped beneath her shoe. Ahead was the creek bank. If she could gain its cover, she might he able to travel along the stream's edge, shielded by the bank itself. The sound of the water would muffle her footsteps.

When she reached within ten yards of the bank, she heard a scraping sound off to her left, like the sound of leather brushing against tree bark. Geneva ran the last few steps and threw herself over the edge, sliding to the bottom in a hail of dirt, exposed dry roots, and small rocks. The cold water closed over her ankles, instantly numbing her feet and taking away her breath.

Looking back, she saw that the bank would truly conceal her. She felt better, she felt hidden. It had been a good plan. It would work.

Feeling some relief from her panic, she started downstream, wading carefully, stepping over the slippery rocks. Her eyes were on the rim of the cut bank, its edge now slightly above the level of her eyes.

It was late afternoon, and the slanting sun fought its way through the tangle of pine and spruce, mottling the rather clear ground along the creek. As she moved, she occasionally encountered an errant patch of sunlight, and the urge was strong to stop and rest within the warmth, for the forest was chilled and all she wore was her thin dress. She had lost her knitted shawl somewhere, snagged on some brush.

The road and her buggy were due west. The road took a curve east before straightening out for the long mile run back into Green Valley from the north. The stream parallelled it until the road swung south, then the stream turned east again, toward its junction with Green Valley. If she could stay with the creek another hundred yards or so, navigating its cover until the road was close, she might be able to elude her pursuer and make a dash for it. Once on the road, she could possibly reach one of the nearby ranch houses.

The stream entered a glade, pastoral and serene. It was such a place she had been looking for when she had left the buggy at the edge of the road and ventured into the woods, a place to pause and daydream.

She pushed on, her feet stumps of ice in the shallow streambed. She grappled with her fears, reasoning that she had heard no further sound of pursuit. Checking her senses, she found she had not even the sensation any longer that he was behind her. Could she have lost him? It was certainly possible.

Her breath came easier. She clambered cautiously from the streambed and made her way toward the road.

Suddenly he sprang from behind a tree and blocked her way. "Well, we had quite a run, didn't we, gal."

Geneva froze, a scream trapped in her throat.

CHAPTER 1

"Twist on it, Christie!" the old man urged.

Christie grasped the horse's tail close to its base and applied all her strength. The mare, on her side now, merely raised her head at Christie and grunted.

"Twist on it, I say. We got to get her on her feet."

"I *am* twisting!" Christie's frustration was near the breaking point. She strained mightily at the mare's tail.

The old man watched, trying valiantly to suppress a grin.

Christie released the mare's tail and straightened up, chest heaving. Her fair face was sheened with sweat and her blond curls were pasted to her forehead. Hands on her hips, she pondered the downed animal.

"Well, *Miss Veterinary Assistant*," said the old man mockingly, "What are we going to do now?"

She glared at him, caught the merry glint in his eye, and compressed her lips into a thin white line.

Wordlessly, she knelt in the dust at the

mare's side and removed one of her spurs. She raised the horse's tail.

"Watch yourself," she warned the old man.

She jammed the sharp rowels into the tender and private flesh beneath the horse's tail.

The mare grunted in pain and surprise, rolled upright, planted her forefeet, and surged to her feet.

Gabe Fletcher stepped aside quickly to avoid being trampled in the rush. Nevertheless, he grinned. "Now that's cogitatin'. I knew if I riled you enough you'd come up with something."

Christie glared again at the old man. The cowhands watching from the fence added to her embarrassment by whooping and applauding.

"You can all go to blazes," she muttered unsmiling as she knelt to replace the spur.

"Don't let yourself drift into a fit of pique," soothed Fletcher. "Good vets have to be able to come up with their own answers all the time. Ask this here mare. She'll tell you you came up with a pretty good one that time."

Bade, the owner of the ranch and the mare, came walking over. "What do you think, Gabe? Is she going to make it? The horse, I mean," he added quickly after a glance at Christie.

"Maybe so — maybe not," replied Fletcher.

"I put all the castor oil down her she could take. Important thing now is to keep her on her feet and keep her moving. Get one of them lazy horse turds on that fence to walkin' the animal. It'll give 'em less time to hoo-rah my girl here." He placed a protective hand on Christie's shoulder. "The mare's to stay on her feet, moving, for twenty-four hours. If she don't die in that time, you can consider her cured."

Bade turned to the men at the fence. "Gordy," Bade called. A short, thin, tow-headed boy froze in his tracks. "Shuffle your tail over here and get to marchin' this mare around the pen. I'll send someone to relieve you in four hours."

Hangdog, the young hand approached and took the lead rope from Fletcher.

He looked worshipfully at Christie. "You did real good, Christie," he said.

Christie, a full three inches taller than the boy, scowled down upon him without comment. He turned meekly and led away the mare.

"How do you suppose that happened, Gabe?" asked Bade. "I've had horses colic before, but usually only in the spring, when the fresh grass hits."

"She's pregnant. You knew that, I suppose," said Fletcher, replacing into his black

12

bag hoses and tubes and various pieces of equipment.

"Hell yes, I knew — she *is* a brood mare." And to Christie, "Beg pardon for my language, ma'am."

"You feeding her any different?"

"Grass has been poor of late. I've been graining all the mares." He looked suddenly thoughtful. "Say, maybe I give her too much too soon, huh?"

The two men walked toward the corral gate, followed by the downcast girl.

"That's my expert opinion, Ed. We won't know until that oil loosens her up. If it's the grain, it'll all come out in the wash. Wouldn't surprise me if she don't lose the foal. Come on, Christie," he said to the girl. "It's late and the old man's hungry."

At the reins of the small black phaeton, Christie asked, "How did you figure it was colic? I would've thought she got into some poison gopher bait or a bad weed of some kind."

Fletcher looked appreciatively at the girl. As he had foreseen, her ill-temper had quickly passed, replaced by the burning curiosity that was so much a part of the young woman's makeup.

Christie's interest in horses and other animals had served her well. In the three years

13

she had been living with the Fletchers, she had acquired considerable knowledge and adroitness in the handling and treatment of ranch stock. She had accompanied Gabe on every call possible, when she felt she could afford the time away from her studies.

Gabe reflected thoughtfully on the blue, questioning eyes locked on his own, waiting for an answer. It was not too unlikely to envision a day, after his own retirement, when Green Valley might have its very first woman veterinary. There was a determination in those eyes bordering on rank stubbornness.

Christie's ultimate plan, once her basic educational requirements were cleared out of the way, was to go on to the university in Denver. That didn't mean her plans couldn't change though. She might decide to stay on and take over from Gabe.

Gabe chuckled and pushed away his wandering thoughts. His mind seemed to do a lot of that lately — straying around like a maverick steer — marching without any apparent order toward feebleness and senility. His chuckle changed to a sad, thoughtful grin.

"What did you say, kitten? That I wasn't listening?"

Christie's eyes, rather than showing impatience, warmed with affection for the old man. "You doddering old fool," she said kindly.

"Pay attention. Good thing I'm driving or you'd lose our way home." She poked him lightly in the ribs with the butt of the driving whip and repeated her question. "What were you listening for with your head pressed against her stomach that way?"

The old man grew businesslike. "When a horse's digestive system is working, its stomach makes a gurgling kind of growling sound. Listen to that crow-bait filly of yours sometime — you'll hear it. Usually it's plenty loud enough. That gurgle means everything is going on as normal. When you don't hear it, then you got troubles. And it's generally colic. Something's plugged up somewheres. With a horse, there's only one way to unplug it — the back door."

The buggy passed beneath rows of cottonwood, leaves shimmering silver in the late afternoon sun. A trickle of water flowed at the side of the roadbed, fed by springs nourished by the snowpack only recently disappeared from the broad shoulders of Grand Mesa. It was Christie's favorite time of the year, when one could look forward to fall's dazzling display of color painted on the west slope. Since leaving the Utah flats she had come to enjoy the variance in color and temperature, the predictable changes one could look forward to in Colorado.

Back in Utah, she had escaped certain death when Marshal Ben Cooper rescued her from the Chambers clan, who had abducted her after they killed the man who had reared her. Hap Hinkle, Christie's adoptive father, had had a sister in Denver who was willing, even eager, to take in the fifteen-year-old girl, but Christie had been through too much to move to a strange place with a woman she had never met.

It was Ben Cooper's lady, Jane Porter, who had given her a home. For a year Christie had lived with the kind and serene woman, working in Jane's diner in Mexican Hat. She had washed dishes and waited tables, and Jane had even begun teaching her the elements of diner cooking.

Paradoxically, just when Christie should have begun to feel content and absorbed in her new life, a vague sadness and discontent stole over her.

She knew the cause. And so did Ben Cooper. On the trail back to Mexican Hat, Christie had been totally honest in confessing her love to Ben. And he had been equally honest in turning her down. Whether from childish infatuation or gratitude, or the first timorous unfolding of real love, she found seeing him with Jane more painful and upsetting with each passing day.

16

One night Jane discovered Christie in tears. After much prodding she persuaded the girl to tell her what was wrong. They agreed that the best way for Christie to regain her own peace of mind was to get away and make a new start.

Jane drafted a letter to her uncle and aunt, Gabe and Vinnie Fletcher, in Green Valley, and the arrangements were made.

The pain of another parting, the upheaval of leaving for a new home, were soon healed by the contentment and security she found living with the Fletchers.

". . . Chances are," Gabe was saying now about the sick horse, "if you can't get her to cuttin' loose like a Christmas goose, you're going to lose her. Guts will rupture. If it gets close to that point, you'll know it, and you'll have to put her down. Can't let an animal suffer needlessly."

Christie thought it over slowly, letting the information sink in.

"You'd better shake a leg," the old man said. "You're still going to that dance, ain't you?"

She gave him a pained look, just short of a grimace. "I *guess* so." She shook her head. "Waste of time. I got studying to do."

Gabe laughed. "You'll break young Steve's heart if you back out now."

17

"I'd like to break his fool head. He's pestered me for months to go places with him. Finally I take pity on him and agree to go to this fool dance, now he's spreading word around that I'm his girl."

"Some gals would figure that a real feather in their bonnet, Christie. Let's not forget Steven Tabor's daddy is one of the well-to-doest mine owners in these parts. Him and Lucius Pike together can likely buy out anyone on the slope, if they've a mind to."

"Shoot," said Christie, "money don't make no one a better person."

"Don't make them worse neither. If their daddy come by it honest."

They rode in silence for a time, lulled by the rhythmic clop of the bay's hooves, the gentle lurching of the phaeton over the hard-packed dirt road.

It was dusk when they reached town. Together they unhitched, and while Gabe fed the bay, Christie tended to her paint filly, giving the animal hay and a perfunctory rubdown.

On their way into the house the old man remarked, "Seriously, Christie, of all your young friends I feel you're safest sticking to them with some substance. Whatever you think of this Tabor kid, I hear he handles himself pretty well, and he's pretty solid in his thinking all around."

At the steps he paused and took her arm. "There's been two gals murdered in the last few months. Whoever the sorry son of a bitch is who did it, I don't want him coming after you."

Christie shuddered. The death of Veda Patterson weighed heavily upon her mind these days, casting a pall over the golden Indian summer. Only two weeks ago, Veda's nude body had been found in the alley behind Cramer's dress shop. Her throat had been crushed, and according to Dr. Valbourg, she had been raped.

Four months earlier, Geneva Hendriks was found murdered in a section of the woods close to town. The nature of the attack had been the same. Sheriff Miles Turner had found the body.

Christie had not been well acquainted with the Hendriks girl — Geneva and her mother had stayed pretty much to themselves. Veda Patterson, however, had been a friend. She was popular with most of the young people of Green Valley. Christie and all her friends had been shocked, angered, and frightened by Veda's brutal murder.

"Tolerate that Tabor boy," Gabe said earnestly. "I don't mean you have to marry the fool. But stay with the crowd, if you

19

got to go out at all."

Christie laced her arm around the old man's. "Don't worry, Gabe. I'll stick with Steve Tabor like he was made of greenbacks — which he probably is."

"I'm serious, Christie. Me and Vinnie would take it terrible hard was anything to happen to you."

Something in the old man's voice caused Christie to look at him. Concern had deepened the lines in his seamed face.

"I'm sorry, Gabe," she said softly. "And I *will* be careful — I promise."

She kissed him tenderly on his wrinkled, white-whiskered cheek, and they started up the steps into the house.

CHAPTER 2

Steven Tabor loomed in the open doorway, tall, blond, handsome, immaculately dressed in a new black suit. His white teeth and his polished boots gleamed.

"Young Mr. Tabor," intoned Vinnie Fletcher solemnly. She pulled him forcefully into the house and closed the door. "No sense tryin' to heat all outdoors," she said without smiling. "And if you don't have this child home by midnight, I guarantee this'll be the first and last time you're awarded the pleasure of her company. Do I make myself clear?"

If Steven Tabor did not find Vinnie Fletcher's tone intimidating, her bulk most certainly did the trick: tall and wide with coarse Slavic features. Her iron-gray hair was pulled back, locked into a tight bun, and held there ruthlessly with two yellowed ivory combs.

"Vinnie," said Gabe, "why don't you run and see if Christine is ready."

At that moment Christie entered the room, decked out in a dress of bright green material. The high collar clung modestly to her slim throat, and the yards of material in the skirt amply disguised her long, coltish legs.

Christie was a pretty girl, not beautiful, but definitely pleasing to the eye. Her fair features bore a quality somewhere between ladylike and tomboyish. In spite of the pressure of Vinnie Fletcher's critical scrutiny, Steven Tabor had the presence to murmur, "You look wonderful, Christie."

She gave him a tolerant but weary smile. "Let's get going and get this over with," she said. "Sooner I get back into everyday clothes the better I'll feel."

They started down the steps to the waiting buggy. Vinnie stood in the doorway, watching them.

"Get back inside here, Vinnie, and let the girl be." Gabe Fletcher closed the door, chuckling to himself. "That Christie, she's a glitter."

The buggy was a sleek, single-seated, impractical affair, employed this night for the obvious purpose of impressing Christie.

"It's brand-new," Steven boasted. "I bought it with money I earned working for my dad this summer. It's made so you can put sled runners on it. We'll have some great rides this winter," he exuded.

"It's nice," said Christie. "Too bad you

couldn't get one with two seats. Now that would *really* be nice." She grinned into the darkness.

"I could've," he answered a bit defensively. "I thought it would be nicer, more private this way."

"Nicer," she agreed, "as long as you're not stuck with someone boring or stupid."

He laughed uneasily and lapsed into a nervous silence, grateful that the trip to the Grange hall was short.

It was a well-turned-out affair. Green Valley was an affluent town, made wealthy by gold and copper mining interests and some of the finest Hereford ranches on the west side. The parents stood about in their fashionable clothes, ostensibly as chaperones, but actually as an excuse for enjoying some socializing on their own level.

Many hours had been spent decorating the hall. Bunting in fall colors festooned the walls. Brass candelabras from the funeral parlor set the light at a golden, ethereal standard, at once holy and yet properly intimate. Glittering crystal punch bowls and cups, and platters of petite sandwiches and nuts burdened tables against the walls.

On a small dais in a corner was the band — piano, banjo, and accordion — earnestly laboring through "Bonaparte's Retreat." A table stood near the door to receive wraps. Once divested, Christie allowed herself to be led to the punch bowl to join one of the small knots gathered there.

"Steven!" exclaimed Joey Pike, in an elegant black suit and a ruffled shirt front. A collar, stiff, white, and new, pressed into a neck bronzed and muscled like that of a young bull. "How did you get Christie to come with *you?*"

Steven beamed proudly at Christie. "She's doing me the honor. Christie, don't pay this outlaw any attention. I'd call him my best friend, except he's always out to stab me in the back — like right now, trying to take my best girl from me."

Christie's smile was fixed. She accepted for a moment the hand extended by Joey Pike, withdrew her own rather quickly, and looked about the room with an air of dismissal.

"Christie!" a tall girl with dark, lustrous hair called to her from beyond the dance floor. The girl left the young man she was dancing with and made her way through the bumping couples to hug Christie. Jennifer Welch was her best friend.

"Lordy, Jennifer," Christie said, "I sure am glad to see you here. I thought for sure I was in for one long evening."

Steven Tabor, at her elbow, blushed but

smiled gamely. "Hi, Jen," he said. "You sure look pretty."

"Hello, Steven," answered the girl.

"Hello, Jennifer." Joey Pike moved into the center of the group and placed a smooth hand on the girl's arm. "Did you come by yourself?"

Jennifer looked startled, and then embarrassed. She smiled and looked about quickly. The young man she had been dancing with stood sheepishly silent behind her.

"Oh Danny," she said to her escort, "I'm so sorry. I didn't mean to desert you!"

"It's all right," he said. "Hi, Christie. It's nice to see you."

He was a pleasant-looking young man with dark, wavy hair that flowed over his collar. He was dressed in a too close-fitting wool suit and roughened boots that had seen a recent attempt at polishing. Strong, calloused, work-ready hands protruded from worn shirt cuffs.

"Jennifer, I'm hurt," Joey exclaimed. "I asked you weeks ago to come to the dance. Now here you show up with Bradstreet." He smiled to show that he was joking, but there remained a hard glint in his eyes as he sized up the other young man.

"Joey," replied Jennifer, perhaps a bit too firmly, "you know as well as anyone that Danny and I have been keeping company. And long before I ever met you."

Pike laughed. "That don't mean you can't move up. You can't find too much class in old farmer boy here."

Jennifer's expression turned to stone. "Quality breeding shows up in many ways, Joey. In manners, for example. I've seen some pretty sorry mules who could outshine you in that department." She turned to Bradstreet. "Come on, Danny. Let's dance."

In spite of the discordant music and the shuffling feet and the conversations from all quarters, a weighty silence settled over the little group while Danny led Jennifer out onto the dance floor.

"Sounds like a good idea," Steven said, rallying brightly. "How about it, Christie? Want to dance?" He gave Joey Pike a sour, sidelong glance and took Christie's elbow, steering her out onto the dance floor.

Christie was not a good dancer. Her natural grace and ease of movement evaporated when forced into the confines of regimented notes and cadences. She felt awkward and embarrassed in the young man's arms. Approximately every tenth step she found herself on the polished toes of Tabor's new black boots. Sweat glistened on her forehead and her freckled nose, and when Jennifer and her partner glided by, Christie cast beseeching eyes upon her friend's laughing face.

"Relax," Steven urged, gallantly trying to steer her about the floor without colliding with other couples. "You'll get the hang of it. You're just too tight. Relax!"

Christie made another half dozen laborious turns, tangled her feet, and lurched sideways.

"To hell with it," she said. "I want some punch." She stalked off the floor, leaving Steven frustrated and mildly embarrassed.

He shrugged helplessly and grinned at those nearby who had witnessed Christie's abrupt desertion, then hurried after her.

By the time he reached her, Christie had procured her punch and was enthusiastically filling a plate with the assorted offerings from the snack tables.

Steven followed suit, maintaining a discreet, inoffensive silence. After a while, he ventured, "Well, it was *kind* of fun, wasn't it?"

She grinned around a mouthful of smoked ham. "No. But if you'll give me a little while to get over my humiliation, we can give it another try."

He laughed and they ate and watched the other dancers, Steven's conversation light and guarded. In spite of Christine Hinkle's eccentric and clumsy social graces, he found her fascinating. His was a campaign to woo this wild and free thing. Since he had first laid eyes on her, he had not had thoughts for any of the other young women of Green Valley. She was special — and very different.

When the musicians took a breather, a number of the dancers stepped outside to cool off in the brisk night air. Lanterns were hung along the wide covered veranda of the Grange building, and couples milled about, searching futilely for darkened corners away from the prying eyes of the adults.

"Here! You youngsters get back up on this porch." Christie recognized the bellowing authority of Jess Harper, a banker and the father of Tillie Harper, one of the miscreants making a break for the shadows.

Christie had no intention of sneaking off into the dark with anyone. She and Steven stood like wooden sentinels directly beneath a lantern near the center of the veranda, and when Steven attempted to hold her hand, she promptly used her other hand to disengage his fingers.

"Christie," he protested. "I really like you. Don't you think —"

"Isn't that the sheriff!" she asked, peering beyond the lamp's glare.

Steven followed her gaze impatiently.

Sheriff Miles Turner was at that moment tying his horse to the hitching rail. He approached the veranda with a slow, measured step.

"Probably checking to see who's drunk," Steven whispered. "Or looking for liquor. Hope he don't look in the buggy."

Christie gave him a sidelong glance, but said nothing.

The sheriff climbed the wooden steps and stood talking for several minutes with Jess Harper. Though Christie was less than twenty feet from the pair, their voices were pitched low and she was unable to effectively eavesdrop. After a while the sheriff moved on inside.

"Let's see what he's up to," Steven said. "He's showing up everywhere lately. Must be looking for that killer."

They reentered the hall. After the cool night air, the atmosphere inside was sweltering and smelled of hot candle wax and sweating bodies.

Christie said she was thirsty, but when Steven poured her another glass of punch, she found the ice had melted and the drink was lukewarm. A mangled lemon rind floated like a dead minnow on the surface.

"If Sheriff Turner wasn't lurking about," said Steven, "I'd go out to the buggy and get something to liven that up for you."

"It's all right," Christie said absently. Her

29

eyes were following the moves made by the sheriff. He was in the far corner of the hall, by the dais, and he was engaged in earnest conversation with Joey Pike. Pike's arms moved in animated gestures. A white-toothed, winning smile dominated his face. The sheriff, Christie noted, was not smiling.

When the lawman left abruptly, Pike crossed the floor and joined Christie and Tabor at their station by the punch bowl.

"What was that all about, Joey?" Steven asked.

"Turner's playing detective again," Pike replied, sneering. "He knew all the mucky-mucks would be here, so he had to put in an appearance. Shows he's on the job, don't you know."

"Why did he want to talk to you?" asked Christie.

Pike shrugged and assumed a modest stance. "Turner's a fishing buddy of my old man. Believe it or not, he wanted to know if I'd seen anyone acting peculiar of late. Can you believe that?" He laughed. "The sheriff of Green Valley turning to me for advice."

"The sheriff asked you for advice?" Christie asked, making no attempt to disguise the skepticism in her tone.

"Happens all the time, my dear," said Joey with a sly wink. He looked at Christie a long moment, his eyes challenging. He obviously expected her to break first, to be the first to look away, but Christie held fast, letting him read in her blue eyes her total disregard for him.

The contest was broken when the three were joined by Jennifer Welch and Danny Bradstreet.

"Danny had a good idea, Christie," Jennifer said. "He's taking me up on the mesa for a picnic Sunday. Do you want to go?"

The tall, pretty girl looked confused for a moment when Christie responded with a pained expression. And then the situation dawned upon her; if Christie accepted the invitation, Steven Tabor would undoubtedly invite himself along.

"Unless you're too busy, that is," she finished lamely, cheeks red. "Oh, good. The band's back. Let's dance some more, Danny."

Bradstreet, mildly confused, allowed himself to be pulled back onto the dance floor.

At the same moment, Joey Pike spotted a girl without a young man, and he quickly crossed the room and petitioned her into dancing with him. The girl agreed readily enough, her eyes flashing brightly at the handsome Joey Pike.

When he was alone with Christie, Steven said, "Say, that picnic sounds like fun. What do you say? We could take the buggy and make a day of it."

Christie shook her head and hoped her face reflected at least a trace of regret. "Aunt Vinnie insists that I go to church with her every week. And then I have to study in the afternoon. Since I help Gabe, I have to study every chance I get. I plan to go to the university in Denver next fall and I have to catch up on all those years of school I missed. You understand."

Though crestfallen he nodded. "Well, maybe we can go for a ride some night next week. Do you think we could manage that? A short one?"

She felt a twinge of guilt. His ardor in the face of all her rejection was pitiful.

"Well, maybe we could leave the buggy behind and just go for a ride. Folly could use a good workout."

CHAPTER 3

"I could stitch it up for you, Mr. Pike," said Gabe Fletcher. "That isn't the problem. Where it's located, right above the chest muscles thataway — hell, the stitches will pull out in a day or two."

"Well, goddamn it, you're the doctor," Pike answered impatiently. "What the hell can we do? She's too expensive a mare to put down."

"Don't recall sayin' nothing about putting her down," grunted Gabe from his stooped position before the mare's chest. "Wicked as the wound looks, it ain't that serious."

The horse was a young brood mare with sleek, graceful lines. She was just into her third foaling season, and Lucius Pike was justifiably proud of her and her get. The previous night, while the dance was taking place, the mare had ripped open her chest on a spike someone had thoughtlessly driven into the wall of the animal's stall.

A rider from the Pike ranch had summoned Gabe Fletcher a little before dawn.

Christie had dressed sleepily and had come along. The late hour of the dance and the sub-

33

sequent short night had sapped her usual pep and wit, but if a call dealt with a horse, she would endure most any inconvenience to be at hand to watch and learn.

"Twitch her up, Christie," instructed the old man. "That's a tender area to work on, and I'll be standing right where she can get at me with them forefeet."

Christie picked up the twitch. Gently she grasped the mare's upper lip and pulled it through the looped chain. The chain itself was affixed to the end of an old broom handle, cut off to about two feet in length. By twisting the handle, she could tighten the chain about the lip. It did not cause the animal much pain to speak of, but it did give the horse something to think about besides what the vet might be doing to another part of its body.

Fletcher mixed a handful of a granulated substance into a small tin pitcher of water. He stirred it thoroughly, dissolving the granules; then, using a clean white rag, he washed the area of the wound thoroughly. Throughout the procedure the mare eyed Christie resentfully but remained motionless under the pinch of the twitch chain.

"This is good stuff," Gabe explained to Pike. "Boric acid. I'll leave you a box of it. Wash the wound twice a day. What it does, it cleans out the pus and the dead flesh, letting new grow. In six weeks' time you won't be able to find a scar."

Doubtfully, Pike looked at the wide gash on the horse's chest. Bits of red shredded flesh clung to the ragged edges of the wound. Christie reversed the twist on the twitch handle, releasing the pressure. She placed a soothing hand on the mare's velvety nose.

"You got yourself a right proud assistant there, Fletcher," said Pike, gazing at Christie appreciatively. "Miss Hinkle, I believe I've heard my son Joey speak of you. Seems right taken with you, he does. Well, I can sure see why."

"Christie pulls her load all right," Gabe agreed, returning materials to the large leather case. "She could make a dang good vet herself one day. But she has plans to broaden her education," he added provocatively.

"Huh," grunted Pike. "Woman don't need no education, as long as she can read a little and write some. How old are you, gal?"

"Nineteen, sir," replied Christie. Gabe, noting the slight flush mounting the girl's cheeks, cast about for a new topic.

Before he could come up with anything, Pike said, "Nineteen. Is that a fact? Well, you best get a move on, little miss. Don't you know the older a woman gets, the harder it is for her to catch her up a husband? Hell, by the time Elmira was your age, she already had our two pups."

Christie's smile was fixed, her voice polite. "Times are changing, Mr. Pike."

"Well now, is that so?" answered Pike. His eyes held an amused but unyielding glint. "Seems to me that's the woman's place. Man has to do his share, puttin' meat on the table. Women ought to do their part too. Not to say a woman can't make a good vet's assistant though, Miss Hinkle."

"Thank you, Mr. Pike." Christie wedged her tongue between her teeth. She cast a glance at Fletcher and found the old man appealing to her with beseeching eyes.

"Come along, Christie," said Gabe softly. "Shake a leg. Frank Fairchild's got a steer ailing. I promised him I'd be out yesterday, but we run out of daylight."

They started for the phaeton, with Pike following closely behind.

"Frank Fairchild," Pike rambled on, "Now there would be a fine fella for you to team up with, gal. That Fairchild's a hard-workin' young man. Let's see, he would be about twenty-eight now, wouldn't he, Fletcher?"

Gabe loaded his bag into the phaeton. "That'll be two dollars, Mr. Pike."

"Two dollars! Goddamn, man!"

"That's with a buck for the boric acid," said Gabe.

Pike reached reluctantly into his pocket and withdrew the money. "It didn't seem like the job took you no two dollars' worth."

Gabe's eyes grew hard. His tone lost the amiable quality he generally used with clients. "Tell you what, Mr. Pike," he said, "give me back that box of boric acid, and then you'll only owe me a buck. Seems a shame, though, to risk a hundred-dollar horse for the sake of saving a buck. But she's your horse."

"No, no," replied Pike hastily. "She's worth it. I didn't mean that. Just took me by surprise, that's all." He handed over the two dollars with a flourish. "Good job you done on her too, Gabe. Damn good job."

Gabe accepted the money and crawled into the buggy beside Christie. She snapped the reins across the horse's rump and they pulled out.

Before they had gone twenty feet, two riders rode in suddenly from behind the wide barn, blocking the way.

"Doc Fletcher. Christie. I thought I recognized that old phaeton. That's a hell of a relic you got there, Doc."

It was Joey Pike, astride a magnificent gelding with stark white stockings. Beside him, on a less impressive mount, sat a girl that

37

looked familiar to Christie. After a moment she recalled seeing her at the dance the night before. Joey and the girl had danced together much of the time.

"Well, Pa," Joey called to his father, "did he get that old hay burner patched up for you? Been my horse, I would've used her for coyote bait."

"You wouldn't do no such thing," said the elder Pike. He grinned proudly at his handsome son. "Where're you two kids off to this morning?"

"Headed for the river," answered Joey. "We might fish some, or we might swim. Can't say. Annie here, she already promised me I could see her in her bloomers."

"Joey!" The girl blushed furiously. "I did no such thing! Mr. Pike, make him quit teasing." Despite the protests, her cheeks were dimpled with pleasure.

"You mind your manners around the ladies, Joe," his father cautioned, with a supportive wink at the girl. "I raised you to be a gentleman, don't forget."

"I know, Pa." He grinned. "But Annie's been tantalizing me all morning. She's got coming whatever she gets." He turned his smile upon Christie. "Have you met Annie Brock, Christie? Her folks moved here from Telluride. Her father's a geologist for the government. She ain't too well acquainted around town yet."

Christie raised a hand in a little wave.

"Christie Hinkle's an orphan," said Joey, lightly joking. "She's staying with the Fletchers — our good veterinarian and his wife — until she's old enough to strike out on her own."

Christie's hands tightened on the reins. She had had enough of the Pikes — father and son — for one day. "We got to go tend that sick cow," she mumbled to Gabe.

"Hey, Christie," said Joey. He made no effort to move his horse from blocking the buggy. "I got a dandy idea. Why don't you go saddle up your paint horse and meet us at the river. Only one thing better than dipping with a pretty girl, and that's dipping with two." He laughed heartily. Annie Brock gave him a strained smile.

Christie scowled. "No, thanks," she said. "I got my work to do. And then I got to study."

She slapped the driving lines hard against the gray's rump. The animal surged forward, brushing aside Joey's mount.

"Some other time," the young Pike called after the carriage.

"It was nice meeting you," faintly pursued the sweet, thin voice of Annie Brock.

Frank Fairchild was a newcomer to the slope. Two years ago he had bought a quarter section of land on the Gunnison River. Located next to open range, his section was a decent spot with good possibilities. He stocked it immediately with fifty head of whiteface Herefords, and in a very short time he had doubled his herd.

Christie recalled visiting the place once before, when Fairchild had called upon Gabe to treat a bull that had been bitten on the nose by a rattlesnake. The bull's nose had swollen horribly and the animal was partially blinded. It turned out to be a frustrating call because there was decidedly little that Gabe could do. However, after a few days the bull recovered nicely on its own, to the gratitude of Fairchild and to the greater surprise of Gabe.

On this morning when they drove into the ranch yard, they found Fairchild riding in from the opposite direction.

He looked grim as he dismounted and approached the buggy.

"Mornin', Gabe." He simply nodded to Christie. He was a tall man with a broad face, a large head, and prominent nose. A smile would have rendered his face pleasant, but now his lips were set and his eyes serious.

"What's the story, Frank?" asked Fletcher. "Sorry I couldn't get out last night."

"Probably wouldn't have done no good if you had. I rode out to shoot her this morning, but she was already dead."

"You don't say so," said Fletcher. "Dropped just like that, huh?"

"Almost. I noticed her acting kind of dauncy three or four days ago. Day before yesterday she starts staggering around a bit — seemed to be having a hard time gettin' her wind. Swelling up a bit under her neck, too."

Fairchild took off his hat and mopped his brow with his bandanna. For October, it was unseasonably warm. Christie noticed that his broad forehead was heavily lined, deeply marked for the face of a young man of twenty-eight.

"Crawl back up on your horse, Frank," said Gabe. "I want to have a look. I don't like the sound of this."

Fairchild nodded. "Neither do I," he said dismally, "neither do I."

They followed him as he led the way north over hilly and sparsely grassed terrain. In a place or two, the phaeton had difficulty, but Christie was able to maneuver around the obstacles.

As they neared the edge of Black Canyon, Fairchild dismounted. Christie and Fletcher crawled from the carriage and followed him as he led the way through a narrow, sage-choked gully. At the far end of the gully flowed a narrow trickle of water. Beside the stream, against a dry clay bank, lay the heifer. "She must've been after water," observed Christie as they neared the downed animal. In the heat of the day, the carcass had already begun to bloat.

Fletcher knelt and inspected the carcass closely. A bloody discharge, dry now, had emanated from the animal's nostrils and anus. About the throat and across the back and flanks had occurred acute swelling, obviously present before the bloat had began.

After a few moments Fletcher stood up. He looked across the carcass at Fairchild, who stood silently, hands in his pockets.

"I think you know what we're looking at as well as I do," said Fletcher.

Fairchild nodded. "Yeah," he answered dejectedly. "I guess I knew it all along." He sighed raggedly. "I was sure hopin' for something else, though."

"I hate to be the one to say it, Frank," Gabe said softly, "but they'll all have to be destroyed."

"What? Do you mean his whole herd?" Christie looked unbelievingly at the dead heifer.

"It's peracute anthrax, Christie," explained Gabe. "He's got no choice."

Christie was stunned. "One cow dies and he has to destroy his whole herd?" The immensity of it staggered her. "You sure the rest have got what she had?"

"We got to act as though they do. It don't hit just one out of a bunch. It infects them all."

He turned back to Fairchild, "Where did you get her, Frank?"

"Bert Montgomery — the horse trader — he told me a fella down in Durango was getting set to pull out. Had about twenty-five head he was letting go for a song. I should've known better," said Fairchild. "I spotted a couple of Texas brands on some of them. They'd probably been in with some of them brought up from Mexico." He turned and launched a kick at the clay bank. "Damn it! I knew better, too!"

Gabe and Christie stood silent, helpless to comfort. Likely, destroying Fairchild's herd would mean the end of the man, at least as far as his efforts here were concerned. Like most ranchers starting out, his entire worth was almost surely tied up in his livestock. He would be left with nothing to build on, nothing to give to the bank.

"There's a good possibility," said Gabe,

"that the fella who sold them to you didn't know they were infected. Anthrax moves fast. In its acute stages it can down a healthy critter in a couple of days."

Fairchild nodded. "What about the hides?" he asked. "I got eighty-five head. That many hides could bring in something at least."

Fletcher shook his head. "We got to burn everything — the entire animal. Everything."

Fairchild stood with his hands on his hips. He looked around in a lost manner, first at the dead cow at his feet, then away to where the terrain began to drop away into the canyon.

"I'll get the word around, Frank," said Gabe. "You'll have help. You won't have to do it all by yourself."

"Obliged for that, Gabe." He took a final look at the cow, let out a weak sigh. "Well, I guess I'd better start combing the brush and pushing them back down to the pens. It'll take most of the day just to gather them."

"You'll have some help out here by this afternoon," Gabe said as they walked back to the carriage. When they reached the phaeton, he added, "Don't get too discouraged, Frank. You're young. You got it in you to bounce back."

As they drove slowly back to town, Christie exclaimed, "What a rotten thing to happen.

44

I feel so sorry for that guy I could bawl."

"Like Frank says, that's the cattle business." Gabe looked gloomily straight ahead.

"But why the hell couldn't it have happened to that horse turd, Pike? That man could stand some hard luck."

Fletcher looked at her, amused. "Lord causes the rain to fall on the just *and* the unjust," he answered mildly. "The horse turds will have their day."

CHAPTER 4

They sat on rocks the size of peach baskets, trailing their bare feet in the icy water. Though it was a warm day, the water was far too cold for swimming, and it churned and dashed between the rocks in an unleashed torrent. If a person lost his footing, he would surely be swept away. It was for this stage that Green River had been named, when the water was dark green, broiling, and treacherous.

But it felt good on Annie Brock's feet, and she wiggled her toes, squinting at the sunlight on the water.

Joey Pike reached out and seized her hand. He laced his fingers between hers, and she smiled at him happily.

"Joey," she said, quite loudly to be heard above the rushing water, "how do you feel about me — really? I know we've only known each other a week or two, and we never spent much time together before the dance last night — but, golly, we seem to get along so well together . . ." She looked at him plaintively.

Annie was experiencing a raging infatuation

for the handsome, dark-haired Joey Pike. She had known no one before who had even come close to Joey's charm, and the way he made her feel . . .

"How do I feel about you?" He cocked his head to one side. "Well, honey, I guess I love you. Guess? Hell, I'm sure of it."

"You do? You are?"

"Well, yes. Of course. I feel every bit the way you do right now." His eyes were warm, and she could see desire in those eyes.

"You feel like I do?" She felt a deep surge of gladness. "Joey, that means that you're my beau."

"I read in a flyer from one of the outfits I get supplies from," Gabe said as they drove slowly through the warm Indian summer afternoon back to town, "that they're in the process of developing a vaccine to fight anthrax. A fella in France, a scientist — Pasteur, his name is — discovered a way to inoculate the beasts with a cultured bacteria. He's been working on it since 'eighty-one and he's durn near got it perfected. According to the article."

"Can people get anthrax?" Christie asked. The image of the bloated heifer had remained with her.

"Yes, honey, they sure can. And sheep, and

horses, and swine. Most grazing critters pick it up off contaminated ground. The manure from one infected animal can infect the entire herd."

"Well, how do humans get it?"

"*That* I'm not too sure about. I would suspect by drinking contaminated milk, or the like. The biggest threat, I do believe, is to livestock.

"When I get home, first thing, I'm going to tell the sheriff what's happened. He'll round up a crowd to give Frank a hand. After that, I'll telegraph the Blackmar company to see if they got any of that vaccine in stock yet. It's too late to do Frank any good, but, who knows, it might cut off a major epidemic."

When they reached town, Gabe let Christie off at the house while he continued on to the sheriff's office.

Christie was not eager to return home. It was early afternoon of a beautiful and warm day, likely one of the last such days she would see on the western slope for many months to come. However, she had studying to do.

"There's a letter for you on the table," called Vinnie Fletcher as Christie entered the room, boots clumping. "And pull them boots off on the porch. I don't want no manure scattered over my clean floor."

Christie retreated to the porch, smiling. She

pulled off her boots, left them by the front door, and tried entering again.

"It's from that marshal friend of yours in Mexican Hat," Vinnie said from the kitchen. "Writes a real newsy letter, when he writes at all."

Christie sat down at the table in the small dining room adjoining the front room. She picked up the envelope and found it had, indeed, been opened.

"Aunt Vinnie," she said loudly to the closed kitchen door. "Will you please quit opening my mail? I'm not a little girl. I'm a grown woman. I would like just once to open a letter for myself."

Vinnie appeared in the doorway, a look of haughty indignation on her broad, heavy features. She marched across the room, staunch hips adroitly navigating the close quarters. She set a plate with a sandwich and a glass of cold milk on the table before Christie.

"Well, I'm sorry," she said tightly. "I didn't know you were so dang touchy. What I thought was we was family. An' families don't have secrets. But I guess I was wrong on that score, as usual."

"I would just like to open my own mail," said Christie, a bit mollified. As usual, when entering a conflict with Aunt Vinnie, win or lose, Christie came off the encounter feeling guilty, whether she was right or not. And there was no real winning with Aunt Vinnie. The woman simply would not fight fair, always assuming the role of the hurt, long-suffering parent. Though Christie readily saw through the ploy, it nonetheless always worked on her, and far too effectively.

Christie sighed and looked at the sandwich with downcast and, what she hoped would appear, repentant eyes.

"All right, Aunt Vinnie," she said sweetly, smiling up at the old woman, "I'm sorry. I didn't mean to bark at you. I'm just a little out of sorts today. You may open my mail any time you want. But please, don't tell anyone but me what's in it. Okay?"

The old woman patted Christie's hand, then stooped and planted a brusque kiss on the girl's cheek. She bustled happily back into her kitchen, leaving Christie in grateful peace.

When she was alone, Christie ignored the food and sat staring at the envelope on the table. After a moment she picked it up. Her fingers trembled. How wildly her heart beat when she pictured the face of Ben Cooper, and those strong, calloused hands that had held these very pages, that had penned the words within — this letter, only the third such that he had written to her since she had left Mexican Hat three years ago.

50

Almost reverently, she extracted the letter from its travel-soiled envelope, slowly unfolded the pages and began to read:

October 15, 1888

Dear Christie,

I take pen in hand to inform you that I am fine and hope this missive finds you the same. Things are pretty much the same here in Mexican Hat. I have fell into a real lazy life, with Deputy Cecil Akins doing most of the work — which galls him no end.

In very truth, I am still a bit under par from the ordeal four years ago. I have not been able to regain much of the weight I lost, and therefore am still somewhat weak. But I would reckon time will solve that situation, as it does most things.

In case you have not heard, Jane was marry'd two weeks ago Saturday. She marry'd a fine gentleman from Durango, where he has a business in men's haberdashery. He is well fixed, or so I understand.

Well, I certainly hope and pray the best for her. She is a wonderful woman and deserves such. I certainly cannot blame her for not wishing to wait on me longer. As you pointed out, Christie, so long ago on that cold, cold desert, something just was not right for Jane and me. I loved her but it was not a strong, holding kind of love that a woman needs to build her life on. At any rate, Godspeed to her and her new husband. And I am sure you feel the same.

You remember my horse, old Doc, the steeldust? Well, I finally retired that old boy. He is taking life easy on old man Macpherson's ranch north of town. I sure feel guilty about all the hard trails I put that horse down during our years together. I thought he deserved to take life easy from —

Christie folded the pages softly. Tears glistened in her eyes as she imagined the gaunt figure of Ben Cooper bunched over these pages, laboring out the letter she now held in her hand.

He would be alone now, except for Cecil. Ben had few close friends. He felt — as he had told her on one occasion — that a job as a lawman left little time for friends. She had thought later that his explanation had been his way of dodging the real problem — his own, at times, crippling shyness.

Christie sat with the closed pages in her hand, staring across the room, lost in the floral patterns of the wallpaper. She wiped her eyes on the napkin Vinnie had brought with her lunch, and thought of Ben Cooper as she had last seen him, standing with Jane Porter on the depot platform in Mexican Hat.

An impulse took hold of her. She would go to him. She would help him. He could not turn her away now. As she had pointed out to Aunt Vinnie, she was no longer a child, she was a woman. Ben needed a woman to care for him.

Even as she held these thoughts to her, her gaze fell upon her stack of books resting on the rolltop desk in the front room.

Her love for Ben was worth everything, every sacrifice. Going to him now would mean giving up her school, giving up her plans for attending the university in Denver; it would mean giving up the dreams she had held close for the last three years.

There was a soft rap on the door. Christie folded the letter and hurriedly tucked it away between her schoolbooks. She wiped her eyes and opened the door.

She was a bit surprised to find Jennifer Welch standing on the porch.

"Are you busy?" asked Jennifer. She wore a worried frown on her pretty face.

"Not especially. Come on in." The truth was, this was the first occasion in their friendship when Christie was not especially glad to see her friend. Her own problems weighed heavily upon her mind. Nevertheless, she smiled and led the way into the dining area.

"Have you had lunch?" Christie asked, indicating her sandwich, untouched, on the table.

Jennifer smiled wistfully and shook her head. "I need to talk to you, Christie."

"Is something wrong?" Christie asked, sensing real concern in her friend.

Jennifer looked nervously at the door leading to the kitchen. They could hear faint sounds of Aunt Vinnie moving about, preparing supper, humming softly.

"She won't bother us," said Christie. "Come sit down." They took seats on the horsehair settee in the front room. "What's the trouble, Jen?"

Jennifer shook her head. "It's Joey. He's been bothering me again."

"Bothering you? How?"

Jennifer's hands were folded tightly, as though to keep them under firm control.

"Last week he came by the house. Mother and Father were both out. I was working in the rose garden, alone. He told me he had made up his mind. I was to be his girl. It was settled, and that was that."

Christie gave a short, sneering laugh. "Oh,

54

he did, did he? And you weren't to have any particular say in the matter?"

She nodded. "I guess not. I told him I was seeing Danny, and I really wasn't interested in him. He laughed when I said that. He said I'd come around. And he said as far as Danny Bradstreet was concerned, he could be squashed like a june bug."

"You let him get by with that? I would have told him to go straight to hell! Why didn't you tell your father?" Christie's cheeks turned red. Her blue eyes snapped with anger.

"You had to see him, Christie. He's strange. I think it's in him to hurt people. And he had that fancy gun he always wears. I was afraid to tell Father — afraid he would confront Joey. And maybe Joey would . . ."

Christie took Jennifer's hands and gripped them. "You can't let a person like Joey Pike push you around. You have to stand up to him, no matter what it costs." As Christie spoke the words, ghost images of the Chambers clan snapped before her like pictures in a nickelodeon; Delwin, with his evil, hungry eyes and his bullwhip; little Frankie, with a killer's heart. "People who do that to women — force them into . . . things, with threats . . . or . . . whips, they're . . . Tell your father, Jen. Or tell Sheriff Turner."

"Christie, if you could see his eyes —"

"Damn his eyes! His eyes can't hurt no one, and neither can he if the sheriff locks him up. You tell your pa. Was that the only time he bothered you like that?"

"Well . . ." Jennifer looked again at the kitchen door. "There was last night at the dance, remember?"

Christie nodded. "I thought you handled him right well."

Jennifer's voice dropped to a whisper. "There's something else," she said agonizedly. "He came to my house this morning — early, just after dawn. No one was up. He came to my bedroom window and tapped on the glass."

"He did what?" Christie's voice raised, and she too cast a quick glance at the closed kitchen door.

"He still had on the clothes he wore to the dance. He wanted me to crawl out the window. I told him no, of course. I wasn't going to go sneaking off with him." She drew a ragged breath. "He got real mad and said he wasn't no farm boy to be teased — meaning Danny, of course. He got so mad, when he left he threw a rock through my window."

"Jen, I hope to God you told your pa this time!"

Jennifer's eyes dropped. Tears welled and coursed down her cheeks. She said nothing.

Christie stood up suddenly. "Come on. This is insane." She pulled Jennifer to her feet and started her to the door. "We're going right to the sheriff with this. Joey Pike has bothered you for the last time!"

CHAPTER 5

Deputy Sheriff Jasper Lockwood listened to the young women in silence. Behind the desk his chair was tilted back on two legs against the wall, and he employed a well-chewed toothpick, worrying it from one side of his mouth to the other.

"Well," he drawled slowly when they had finished recounting Jennifer's latest incident with Joey Pike, "the sheriff definitely will hear of this. Right now he's out with Doc Fletcher, supervisin' the shootin' of Fairchild's herd. Damn shame, that." He shook his head. "Fine fella like that. Real pity. Wonder how a disease like that gets started. Bet it's in the water. You girls be careful you drink only clean water, ya hear?"

"Deputy Lockwood," Christie said impatiently, "we want someone — either you or the sheriff — to tell Joey Pike to stay away from Jennifer."

"Well, yes. I could do that," Lockwood replied agreeably. "No problem. I was just thinkin' it might have more weight, though, comin' from Sheriff Turner."

Christie smiled at him encouragingly. "Oh, I think Joey would listen to you, Deputy. Green Valley is lucky to have two such professional lawmen."

"Well, that's mighty nice of you to say so, Miss Hinkle. Mighty nice indeed."

On the dusty street, Christie said to Jennifer, "Why don't you spend the night at my house? I don't think Joey will pester you anymore, but just in case. We can have Martha Cryor come over too."

The worry in Jennifer's eyes lifted as the girls walked down the plank walk, chatting happily. As they passed the Green Valley blacksmith and livery, they encountered Danny Bradstreet, emerging from the barnlike structure with a long logchain coiled and draped across his wide shoulders.

The young man looked pleased and embarrassed at the same moment. His face was dusty, tanned, and when he smiled his white teeth showed up in sharp contrast.

"Hi, Jen. How are you, Christie?" His voice was soft and gentle.

"Hi, Danny." Jennifer flashed a radiant smile of her own. "What are you doing in town?"

"Dad and me were worryin' out some stumps. Broke the old chain a couple of times. Figured I'd come to town and buy a new one.

I'm glad I did — if I hadn't come in, I wouldn't have got to see you until tomorrow."

The two exchanged looks that made Christie feel like an eavesdropper.

She wondered if Jennifer had shared with Danny the nature of her problem with Joey Pike. No, she thought not. Christie noted Bradstreet's thick, muscled arms, beefy shoulders, and chest. *This is one bug I would like to see you squash, Joey Pike.*

"You know, Jen," Danny said with an embarrassed glance at Christie, "I was just thinking, if you're not busy tonight, they got a travelin' magician puttin' on a show down at the Blue Swan diner. Maybe we could stroll down and take it in."

Jennifer looked quickly at Christie. "Oh, Danny, I'd really love to, but you see Christie and I —"

"Go on," Christie said quickly. "You can spend the night at my place anytime, Jen."

"Come with us, Christie," urged Jennifer. "That would be all right, wouldn't it, Danny?"

"Sure," answered Bradstreet. "My treat. Maybe your friend Tabor would like to go, too," he suggested.

Christie shook her head adamantly. "No. You two go. I've got a lot of studying to do."

She was able to convince the pair that staying home was what she wanted to do, and so it was left at that.

After making arrangements for meeting Jennifer later, Danny left them, and the girls continued down the street.

Before they parted at Jennifer's house, Christie warned her, "If Pike shows up and causes any trouble, you go to the sheriff. And if that doesn't work, let Danny have a go at him. I think if a person ever got Bradstreet good and mad, that sorry individual would be looking for a hole mighty quick."

When Christie reached home she changed from her dress to her denim pants, her favorite old shirt, and boots. She stuck Ben Cooper's letter in her pocket and went out the back door to saddle her horse.

Christie kept her paint filly, the foal from her mare, Dulcie, in the small barn and fenced paddock behind the house.

During her time of captivity with the Chambers clan, Christie had given up hope of ever seeing the little horse again. Ben Cooper, upon finding the dynamited wreckage of Christie's and Hap Hinkle's cabin, had discovered the foal and had taken the little animal to old Simms, who kept it until Christie reclaimed it.

She let the filly reach the age of three years before she broke the animal to ride.

While still in Mexican Hat, she had continued to pamper Dulcie, the old mare, making up with loving kindness and good hay and grain for the suffering the animal had undergone during the period of Christie's captivity. When she left Mexican Hat, she had left the mare with Deputy Cecil Akins.

"My Sunday horse," Akins had declared with a wink at Ben Cooper. "Don't you worry about her none, Christie. She an' I are going to ease into retirement together."

After Christie came to Green Valley, Gabe had borrowed an old buckskin for her to ride until the paint filly was trained. It took her three months to accomplish that task, working in her spare time from studying and from helping Gabe. When finished, the paint was a duplicate of its mother, temperamentally sound, easygoing, and a horse that was a genuine pleasure to be around.

On the way out, Christie had snatched a carrot from a box on the back porch, and she offered it now to the filly, along with kind words and a judicious amount of patting and stroking. "It always pays to get on the good side of a young horse before you get on its top side," Hap had always told her. When she had the horse saddled, she rode to the edge of town at a gentle canter.

A half hour later found her threading her

way through jack pine, mountain laurel, and frequent deep swatches of quaking aspen. The leaves of the aspen made a brilliant shimmering golden splash against the side of the mountain, framed in greens, burnt orange, and deep browns.

A stream gurgled off to her left, and she followed it up the side of the mountain.

Eventually she came to a rock ledge, lichen-covered and cool, overlooking the stream. The water was sparkling to the eye, and when she knelt to drink, it was so cold it made her teeth ache and her chin numb.

It was a beautiful spot to which she had come, a place she visited often during troubled or sad times. Today she needed this place, for her heart was heavy and confused.

She tied the filly's reins to a branch and took a seat on a large rock jutting out into the stream. The air was chilly but the sun had warmed the rock, and she pulled off her boots. After one foolhardy thrust of her feet into the icy stream, she sat back, content to bask in the healing sun and shadow moods of the forest around her.

After a time she pulled Ben Cooper's letter from her pocket, reread it several times more, pondered its helplessness, weighed its voiceless and unintentional plea.

What would Ben say if he guessed what she

was considering? Christie gave the brook a sad little laugh. He'd forbid her to return, to sacrifice her plans for his sake. She would need to remind him that at one time *he* had been the sum of all her plans and dreams. Because of him, she was alive to have those dreams. And because of Ben Cooper, she had the courage and the confidence to go after them.

It was true, more than likely, that if she returned to Mexican Hat, those plans were at an end. Could she accept that?

Now just a minute here, Christine, she lectured herself from her rocky podium, we've already decided that Ben is worth it all, worth giving up everything for, even your life. Isn't that what love is about — putting aside all selfishness for the sake of the loved one? Well, isn't it?

She bounced an angry stone off the far bank and unfolded the letter again.

He had included a paragraph on Lame Badger, the Ute who had very nearly proved their undoing after Ben had rescued her from the Chambers gang. "They brought Lame Badger to trial, finally," he wrote,

for the murder of three men and a woman from the Willow Creek Agency. Christie, can you belief this? They let him go.

You heard me talk of my old friend Amos

Crabtree, the marshal at Fort Sill? He was at the trial. He figures the reason was the public was tired of the whole Ute question. The big shots in Washington just want things laid out and forgot. Heck of a world, ain't it, gal?

At the end of the letter, Ben made a few comments on the weather, a few more on Deputy Cecil Akins, and signed off. Not once had he intimated that he needed Christie, that he wanted her to return to Mexican Hat. It was all in the letter except that: the brokenness, the intense loneliness, the wistful longing for something life had denied him; that something which now, Christie felt, only she could provide.

She was weeping when she returned the letter to its envelope, her heart torn by the renewed pain she thought behind her.

The paint filly wickered. The horse had eaten all the pine needles within reach, and now she looked at Christie with large, inquiring eyes.

Christie pulled on her boots and got slowly to her feet. She felt a great weight rested on her narrow shoulders. She must decide. Should she return to Mexican Hat? Would he reject her again? Or would he welcome her with love and gratitude?

She returned the letter to her pocket, mounted the paint, and rode slowly down the path through the pines.

CHAPTER 6

The next day, Sunday, it rained. Christie decided not to go to church. After a lazy breakfast, she slogged out to the barn and gave the paint a thorough grooming. Outside the rain fell in an unrelenting downpour, and there was a light wind.

But inside the stall it was cozy and warm and peaceful, with the pungent smell of hay and manure. The filly radiated a tremendous amount of body heat, and the girl stood close to the animal as she brushed and labored over its already immaculate coat.

When the horse was pampered to her satisfaction, Christie picked up the manure fork and went to work mucking out the stalls.

It was noon when she finished her labors, but she was feeling better, about herself and about the world. Now, with much of her unrest worked out on the handle of the manure fork, she felt she might that afternoon be able to concentrate on her books.

When she opened the door onto the back porch, she was attacked by the smell of frying chicken. Instantly she was famished, and she pulled off her muddy boots, slipped out of her soaked coat, and crept into the kitchen in hopes of stealing an advance piece from under Aunt Vinnie's watchful eye.

The kitchen was empty. Great luck, she congratulated herself. And then she heard voices from the front room: Gabe and Vinnie, and one voice with which she was not at first familiar — a man's voice, deep and serious sounding.

She quickly finished off the chicken leg, wiped the incriminating evidence from her lips and fingers, and passed through the door into the front room.

Gabe sat in his chair, sockless and relaxed, Vinnie in her rocker, rocking, as she did everything else, in a relentless, business-only manner. On the horsehair sofa sat Sheriff Miles Turner. A cup of coffee was balanced on one knee. His rain-soaked hat was on the floor, brim side up. Even his long, drooping mustache looked soaked, like the whiskers of a gopher emerging from a flooded burrow.

At the mustache his frivolous appearance ended. His eyes were stern and appraising, peering out from beneath heavy brows that bore a continual questioning arch. He was a large man, in his late thirties, possibly, a bit inclined to an early paunchiness, but still with a settled strength in his broad shoulders and heavy arms. The hands that manipulated the coffee cup were large and powerful looking.

When Christie entered the room, the sheriff set his cup on the floor next to his hat and stood up in an awkward, clumsily genteel manner. He nodded at the girl, and broad, horsey teeth showed in a smile through the soaked brush of his mustache.

"Sheriff," said Gabe, "this is Christie Hinkle. I guess you could call her our daughter, of sorts." There was something in the old man's voice when he spoke those words that touched Christie and made her feel instantly warm. She gave the old man a loving smile before she turned to the sheriff.

"We've not met — not officially, Miss Hinkle," said Turner, "but I've heard many good things about you."

"I'm pleased, Sheriff. Thank you." She sat down on a hard-back chair near the heating stove. The sheriff resumed his seat and retrieved his coffee cup.

"As a matter of fact," said Christie, "my friend Jennifer and I were by your office yesterday. Did your deputy mention it?"

"That is one of the reasons I dropped by," said Turner. He took a sip of coffee and stared long into the cup, either judging the quality of the porcelain or solemnly framing his thoughts.

"Jasper said you and Jennifer were a bit concerned over the unwanted attentions of Joey Pike."

Christie looked at the sheriff steadily. "I found out yesterday that Joey had been pestering Jen for weeks. It was my idea to come and see you about it."

The sheriff nodded. "Joey's been something of a burr under my blanket for some time now. I've talked to him repeatedly about his attitude toward the young ladies, but everything I've said's been like so much water off a duck's back. I gather he feels that because his father's rich, he's somehow exempt from proper behavior."

"If you know Lucius Pike at all," interjected Gabe, "you can see where the boy gets that opinion of himself."

"It's not like when I was a girl," put in Vinnie. "In them days a young man did not even come to see a young lady without her parents or some other grown-up person in the room. Now — hell's afire — these youngsters go runnin' off in the woods in all directions. Can't keep track of 'em. Half the time you don't know who they're with." She finished with an accusing glance at Christie.

"Christie ain't prone to that kind of funny business," defended Gabe stoutly. "I'd trust Christie no matter where she's at or who she's with." He turned to his wife. "And, Vinnie, you ought to be ashamed for implying otherwise."

"Wha . . . I . . . ," sputtered Vinnie. "Why you ornery old scudder! I never applied nothing. You're the one always pacing the floor, wandering where she's at. 'Specially when she takes it in her head to take off on one of them rides of hers."

Gabe was on the point of an angry reply when the sheriff, grinning, interrupted. "Folks, please. We're gettin' off the track a mite."

Gabe and Vinnie looked threateningly at one another, but fell silent. The room resumed its somber tone.

"I don't want this to go any further than just us in this room," said Turner. "You all understand that?"

Cristie, the old man, and his wife nodded their heads in unison.

"You're aware," said Sheriff Turner, "of the trouble we've had gettin' a handle on the killer of those two girls. I have . . ." He paused. "I got to be real careful here, how I say this. I see a connection, I believe, between those murders and a certain someone in our community."

"You mean Joey Pike," Vinnie said flatly. "You don't need to beat around the bush, Sheriff."

"Now, I didn't mention a name," Turner said quickly. But each one in the room noted that the lawman made no move to deny it either.

The man was a careful politician, Christie judged.

"If you're wondering, Miss Hinkle, why I'm bringin' my speculatin' to your doorstep, it's because you yourself are a very active and respected part of this here younger community of ours. And I think you got savvy a lick or two above most kids your age. I heard about your ordeal a while back. Them things generally either breaks a person outright or strengthens 'em up like an old oak stump."

"Christie don't take no sass," said Vinnie. If the relevancy of her comment was lost upon the others, it did not diminish the sudden pride in the look she flashed at the girl.

"Let me ask you, Christie," said the sheriff, "Did you know the two murdered girls?"

Christie nodded. "I didn't know Geneva Hendriks that well, but Veda Patterson was my friend."

"Do you know if Joey knew and spent much time with either of the girls?"

The room grew suddenly chilled. Christie looked down at her wet socks. She had left her damp and muddy boots on the enclosed back porch. She shivered.

"I really couldn't say if he spent time with Geneva. I never saw them together. As I told you, I didn't know her well. Joey and Veda did go places together once in a while."

"But you're not sure about the first girl?"

"No, sir."

"Uh huh." Sheriff Turner leaned back and folded his hands across a small potbelly. "Do you know this new girl, Annie Brock?"

"I saw her for the first time Friday. There was this dance at the Grange hall. I didn't actually get to meet her until yesterday."

"And where was that?"

"At the Pike ranch. I was out there with Gabe. She and Joey were riding off somewhere."

Turner looked at Gabe, and the old man nodded affirmation.

Christie held her breath. The sheriff was building to something.

"You wouldn't happen to know where they rode off to, would you?" The expression in his wide eyes grew intense.

"I'm not sure," Christie said. "I think the river, because Joey invited me to go swimming with them."

"Swimming?" said Vinnie. "In this weather? Why, gal, you'd freeze up like a chunk of ice."

"I didn't *go*, Aunt Vinnie," Christie an-

73

swered impatiently. "I just said they asked me. As cold as the water is, I doubt if they went swimming either."

Gabe Fletcher was looking at the sheriff closely. "Why the interest in this Brock gal, Miles?" he asked.

"Got a visit from her father this morning," said the sheriff. "Just after daybreak. Seems she never made it home last night."

"She never came home at all?" asked Christie. "Did you check with Joey?"

Turner nodded. "Went there first thing. Kid was still abed. But see, he had taken her home fairly early. And it checks out. Apparently she had supper with her folks. About six-thirty she headed out the door again. Told her ma she was going over to a girlfriend's house to look at some dress material, or some such. That's the last anyone's seen of her. I went to see the girlfriend — Ella Blanchard. Do you know her?"

Christie shook her head.

"Didn't figure you did. She's fairly new to town, same as the Brock girl. Anyways, Annie never showed up at the Blanchard house. Her pa went over there about three this morning. Got all them folks out of bed with his rantin' and ravin'."

"You suspect foul play?" asked Gabe.

"Got to. And I figured I'd better start with

74

the last people she spent time with."

Gabe looked thoughtful. "So you're tryin' to tie Joey in with the disappearance of the girl."

Turner looked at him evenly. "I'm not tryin' to tie anybody in with it. I'm proceeding on the only logical course I got. Besides her folks, the only person she spent time with yesterday was Joey Pike. And what Christie here just told me would seem to further bear that out. We've searched the town over this morning — Deputy Lockwood and me — and turned up nothing."

He turned on the settee to face Christie. "I'm a firm believer in back trackin'. What do you say you an' me take a ride down to the river. You could show me where the young people are most likely to go these days."

Christie nodded. "Okay. Let me get my boots on."

Before stepping from the barn into the rain, the paint filly looked over its shoulder at Christie, as though to question her judgment in venturing out in such foul weather.

The sheriff, in a tattered slicker, sat his horse, awaiting the girl at the front of the house. Together they rode off through the rain, smoke chugging from the horses' nostrils.

At the edge of town the road branched —

one side leading northwest to Grand Junction, the other northeast, to Cedar Grove and Grand Mesa. They took the branch east, crossed the wooden bridge over the river, turned off the main road, and continued along the river on a narrow logging road. A wagon would have found the road impassable; deep, mud-choked ruts twisted through thick brush and brief, emaciated stands of lodge pole pine.

On one sweep of the river, a natural stone bulwark slowed the water to a walk, and around the resulting pool cottonwoods clustered about a thick ancient oak. On warm summer days the area was ideal for picnics and larks. During the colder months, when the snows were heavy on the mesa, one found evidence of deer and elk laying up among the sheltering trees. There was an abundance of willow and aspen along the banks at this point, excellent forage for the heavier animals.

Just as the horses passed into the trees, the rain, as Vinnie had predicted, turned to snow, large moist flakes that clung to their shoulders and hats. It quickly covered the horses' wet manes and backs, melted, and ran off in tiny rivulets beneath the horses' bellies.

They rode through the trees, wet leaves slapping their faces, saturating their legs.

At last Christie pulled up. "This is the only place I've ever been along this part of the river," she said. She indicated the relatively free shoreline, the large rocks just right for basking upon in the sun.

"Ordinarily the water runs pretty still here," she explained. "Except when they have a lot of rain high up. Then it gets like it is now. I've seen it change in a few minutes' time."

Turner crawled stiffly from the saddle, stretched his wet legs, and looked about dismally. "Well, if a fella was lookin' for tracks he'd be out of luck. Likely we won't be seein' the ground again until spring."

Indeed, the snow was piling up at an unbelievable pace. A half inch had already accumulated on the ground.

The sheriff walked around, hands thrust through slits in the slicker into his pants pockets beneath.

Christie sat the paint for a while, then, feeling chilled, she got down and walked around for warmth. Her feet felt like senseless blocks of wood, and the tips of her fingers ached with the cold. She hoped the sheriff had something constructive in mind, other than passing the time standing around in the snow. A hot tub and a good hot dinner of fried chicken beats this all holler, she declared to herself. Her stomach answered with a low growl.

Turner moved off upstream, checking as he

77

went the clusters of brush, the dark areas beneath the trees.

Christie shrugged. At least it was something to do. She set off downstream, looking for she knew not what. Something, she guessed, anything to indicate the missing girl had been in the area.

She trailed along the edge of the river, walking carefully, lest her foot slip on the wet rocks and dump her into the icy water. She looked at the swiftly moving dark green water and shivered. It would likely mean the end of anyone who fell into the river when it was in this mood — turbulent, angry, lashing at the rocks with white fists.

When she saw the body she thought at first it was driftwood snagged between the rocks, so white were the bare limbs and torso. The head was beneath the water. Eyes wide and staring, staring up, into her own, screaming at her from a bone-white face. Long, auburn hair was pulled in flowing streams with the fierce current.

"Sheriff," she said softly, her eyes locked on those of Annie Brock. She screamed, "Sheriff!"

CHAPTER 7

Martin Valbourg, doctor and coroner, was an effete young man with large, moist eyes and a habit of sniffing, as a sufferer from chronic sinus problems might do. His life in Green Valley was harried and unfulfilling, not at all what he had in mind when he took up the notion of medicine. His days and nights were filled with cranky ranchers and townspeople; people who were slow to pay their bills; long, cold drives in the middle of the night; and a sense that practically all he did was totally without efficacy. Most of his patients, he felt somehow, healed themselves. At times he felt useless. Apart from his setting an occasional broken limb, extracting a defective appendix, the medicine and advice he doled out seemed perfunctory, at times silly, administered to give those well-off miners and ranchers something to talk about over their tea.

He looked at the body of Annie Brock, lying so still upon the table. This task, to examine the girl and to determine the cause of her death, was especially distasteful to Valbourg, for he had known Annie Brock; had, in fact, escorted her to the dance at the Grange on Friday. Though acquainted with her only a few days Valbourg had decided immediately to court her, marry her.

That enchanting little dream had flown away on swift wings when, at the Grange, Joey Pike had asked her to dance and had then spirited her away completely. He had driven home alone in the rented buggy, humiliated, totally dispirited, wishing upon Joey Pike and Annie Brock a host of evils that he would shamefully recant the next morning.

Now, here she lay, as though malevolent ears had heard his curses and a murderous heart had exacted his judgment.

He sniffed, reached for his handkerchief, pulled back the sheet, and set about his examination.

Sheriff Miles Turner squinted at the paper form in his hand. "What does *petechiae* mean?" he asked. His voice was edged with impatience.

"Tiny hemorrhages," Valbourg answered distantly.

"For God's sake," Turner said, exasperated. "Could you just put all this in English? Why the hell do you people always have to make everything so goddamn complicated?"

Valbourg, somewhat embarrassed, pulled

80

his eyes away from the body and turned them meekly upon the lawman.

"Showers of tiny pinprick hemorrhages. In cases of strangulation they occur in the face, in and around the eyes. There was extensive damage to the laryngeal structure. I would say this was done by someone with very strong hands."

"Do you think, *in your judgement*, that this girl was killed by the same individual, or persons, who killed Veda Patterson and Geneva Hendriks?"

Valbourg looked thoughtful. "I believe so," he said after some moments. "Let me put it this way — I've not seen anyting so far to indicate a departure from that premise."

Turner sighed, gave him a pained look. "Well, there's one sick son of a bitch running around out there." He pushed himself tiredly to his feet. "Kind of makes your skin crawl, don't it?"

Valbourg's agreement was a silent one, but as the sheriff reached the door, he asked, "How did her folks take it?"

"How do you think? The mother's heart's broke. The girl's father wants to string up everybody, including me. Thinks I should've got the bastard before he got to his daughter. Hell, I don't blame Brock. After he's had some time to get over the shock he'll cool down.

If he don't do something stupid in the meantime."

"From what I've been hearing, Sheriff, there might be several more citizens contemplating something rash."

Turner opened the door. "I can't let that kind of talk worry me none. People have been doing stupid things long before I ever became sheriff." He began buttoning up his coat. Outside it was snowing in earnest. "Now, if you'll excuse me, Doc. I'm going to pay a visit to a certain young man."

"Terrible about that girl, Miles. I mean, my God, she was such a sweet thing." Lucius Pike looked genuinely shocked. "Why, she was just out here on Saturday. Her an' Joey spent most the whole day together. Ain't that right, Joe?"

Joey was seated as close to the large stone fireplace as he could pull the chair. He seemed undisturbed by the news of the death of Annie Brock.

"I heard you and Miss Brock spent some time at the river," said Turner, strolling over and standing over the chair in which Joey's lanky body lounged.

"That's right." Joey's face was serious, but not serious enough to suit Turner. "We were going to go swimming. Sort of a daredevil thing, but the water was too dang cold. Swift

82

too. It had been raining on the mesa, and that water was *cold*. Freeze the balls off a brass monkey."

"What time did you leave the river?"

Joey's brow wrinkled. He looked at the clock on the mantel above his head. "Right around four, I guess. Maybe a bit later. I think I got her home about five-thirty or six."

"That'd be about right," Lucius Pike agreed. "You must've come in the back door here about six-thirty to supper. Your ma wanted to hold supper, but I told her to hell with that. You come in late, you eat cold vittles."

Turner seemed to consider the older Pike's statement, nodded, turned his back to the fire, and clasped his hands behind him, extending them toward the heat. He looked about casually. It was a large room, in a large house — lavishly furnished rooms with dizzyingly high ceilings. And cold. There was an ever-pervasive chill that quickly soaked into the body and bones of all who entered and stayed for any length of time. The fireplace, it seemed, did little to dispel the chill.

Sheriff Turner looked again at Joey. He smiled in a friendly way. "What did you do Saturday night, Joey?"

Without flinching, Joey answered, "I was home all night, Sheriff."

"Now, Sheriff," said Lucius Pike, "I hope you ain't implyin' my son had anything to do with that girl's death. Why, can't you see how broke up he is about it? Joey tells me things were gettin' pretty serious between the two of them."

"Pa," Joey said with an easy grin, "you know that ain't true. I never said no such thing. You don't have to lie for me."

Turner faced the elder Pike. "I ain't one for implyin' Lucius. I generally come right out and say what's on my mind — as long as it suits my purpose." The sheriff's backside was baked. He turned about to toast the front.

"I am a bit troubled, though," he continued, "by the fact that you two seem to be all set with an alibi for Joey. And not even a glimmer between you. Maybe like you've been doing some rehearsing."

"Or telling the truth," put in Joey.

"Add to that the fact that you just don't seem as broke up as, say, I might be, under the same circumstances. It does get a fella to wondering."

Joey laughed softly. "You want to see me a shattered wreck." He put his arms above his head and stretched lazily. "Sheriff, I'm not an emotional man. I'll grieve Annie in my own way. But I ain't goin' around with my chin dragging the ground, or shedding crocodile tears. That ain't my style. I'm being truthful all the way. Isn't that what you want, Sheriff?"

"You know it is, Joey," said Turner amiably. "But if it turns out it isn't the truth, I'll find out. And when I come back I won't be so calm and reasonable." He walked to the door, his boots echoing hollowly on the hardwood floor.

"We lost three fine young women to some crazy bastard. He looked first at Joey, then at Lucius Pike. "Mark my words, gentlemen, it's going to stop. And soon."

Howard Brock wandered aimlessly about the living room. He regarded the walls, the new furniture, the pictures they had bought for their new home in Green Valley, all those things that he, Louise, and Annie had together picked out. He passed a shaky hand over his eyes and sat down on the edge of the brocade-covered settee. Immediately he stood up and resumed his restless wandering.

His course led him without thinking upstairs to her room, where Annie had planned and worked so industriously, fixing the room to her taste. It was a room where she and her new friends could go to chat away an afternoon, to share those secret things so important to girls on the edge of young womanhood, to marvel over the start of an adult life with grown-up opportunities and responsibilities.

Brock sat on the edge of the bed. The down comforter was pulled smooth and straight, corners square. He rubbed a hand over the tufted material and reflected how the things his daughter had planned for this room, and for her young life, would never be.

He walked to the dresser and picked at the array of combs, brushes, ribbons, the small wicker bowl full of pinecones she had collected on her first walk in the forest behind the house.

Centered on the dresser top was a tintype portrait in a gilt frame of himself and Annie's mother, taken on their wedding day.

As he stood looking at the little things that had been meaningful in Annie's life, he heard a sound through the open door. It emanated from down the hall, from the bedroom he shared with Annie's mother.

He stepped from his daughter's room and closed the door softly, following the sound down the carpeted hallway.

Louise Brock lay on the bed, moaning softly. Her eyes were covered with a cold washcloth that he had wrung out and placed there earlier. He could not tell if she was awake or merely moaning in her sleep, as she had taken to doing since the doctor had given her the laudanum.

He watched her for a moment, decided not to disturb her, then turned and softly stepped from the room.

Downstairs, he resumed his wandering. He stopped in the kitchen, poured himself a cup of coffee he didn't want, left it forgotten on the table while he returned to the living room, again to pace like a caged lion.

The ship's clock chimed four o'clock. Brock started as though someone had fired off a gun. He looked out the window. Still daylight.

He moved to the foyer, slipped into his heavy overcoat, pulled his wool hat over his ears, and left the house just as the first snowflakes of the new storm began to fall.

The main street of Green Valley lay in a breathless lull, awaiting the storm that hung like a great gray blanket above the west slope. The temperature had dropped during the afternoon, and now the puddles of standing water in the street grew feathers of ice at the edge. Brock's heavy shoes clumped hollowly on the frozen ground.

When he reached the sheriff's office, dusk had begun to settle. The snow had piled up on his shoulders and hat.

Deputy Lockwood had lit the two lamps and was just stoking up the small coal heater when Brock entered.

The deputy nodded. "Howdy, Mr. Brock.

87

Cold enough for you? I was over Fort Collins three years ago — started out feelin' just like this. Turned out to be one of the coldest winters on the east side in the last twenty years. Froze thousands of cattle."

"Is the sheriff around?" asked Brock. He refused a cup of coffee the deputy poured and held out to him.

"You just missed him. He's out tendin' to sheriffin' business. Should be back pretty soon, if you want to wait."

"Do you know if the sheriff has made any headway?"

Lockwood looked puzzled. "Headway? Oh, you mean on the . . . on your daughter's thing." He sat at the desk and his face assumed a professional seriousness. "Well, Mr. Brock, I really shouldn't be disclosin' nothing like that."

Brock thrust his nervous hands into his pockets, paced the room, looked out the steamed windows at the gathering darkness.

He turned suddenly upon the deputy, his anguish and his anger stamped on his haggard features. "Deputy Lockwood, can't you tell me anything? I'm going out of my mind. Someone murdered my daughter — my little girl — and I've got a right to know if something's being done about it!" He placed heavy hands on the desk, leaned over the deputy, half imploring, half threatening.

"Why, Mr. Brock . . . I . . ."

"Please! Anything! Just something to live for. Something to think about besides Annie lying dead!" His last words were a choked whisper. His eyes filled suddenly, and tears of frustration trickled down his stubble-covered cheeks as he grabbed the deputy's lapels.

"Well —" The deputy coughed, made an exaggerated show of clearing his throat. "Well, Mr. Brock, it might help you to know we got us a suspect."

"A suspect?" Brock's voice was almost a whisper. He released Lockwood's shirt and straightened up.

"Well, hell yes. Big one, too." He looked guardedly at the door and lowered his voice. "Sheriff's got reason to believe the Pike kid might be involved."

Brock's eyes widened. "Joey Pike? Why, he and Annie — why, they were friends." His jaw muscles grew slack and his mouth hung slightly ajar.

Lockwood nodded. After another glance at the steamy windows he continued, "Turns out Joey might've been close friends with the other murdered gals too." He again looked at the door.

"Joey Pike killed Annie." It came from Brock's lips as a reverent litany. "Joey Pike.

And the sheriff went to arrest him."

"Now, hold on, Mr. Brock," said Lockwood. "I never completely said Joey did it. And I never said the sheriff was goin' to arrest him. You're jumpin' the gun here."

"But if he did it, he has to be arrested." Brock was adamant. He had found a focal point for his pain.

"That's just what I'm tellin' you, Mr. Brock. We don't know for sure he did it. The sheriff just has an eye on him."

Brock appeared not to be listening. He kept repeating the name, *Joey Pike,* whispering it over and over. A chant.

"Uh, Mr. Brock, I wonder if you could maybe keep it under your hat what we been talkin' about here. The sheriff, you know he'd take an inch off my butt side if he found out I said something. Official business, you know."

Brock stared out the night-filled window.

"You won't say nothin', will you, Mr. Brock?"

The sound of boot steps outside brought panic into the deputy's eyes. "Please, Mr. Brock, let's just keep all this about the Pike kid between you an' me, huh? You'd be doin' me a big favor."

Brock reached and opened the door. "Sheriff," he said as Turner entered, shoulders and hat laden with snow, "where is he? Where is the Pike kid? You arrested him, didn't you?"

Turner paused in the open doorway. As he slowly brushed snow from his shoulders, he eyed Howard Brock and then the white-faced deputy. Turner closed the door, hung up his coat and hat, and took the chair behind the desk hastily vacated by Deputy Lockwood.

"What's going on here, Jasper?" he asked of the deputy, his eyes on Brock.

Brock answered. "Your deputy says Joey Pike killed Annie. Where is he? Why haven't you arrested him?"

"Because we have no proof he did it," Turner answered. His tone, while not unkind, was firm. "I'm afraid Jasper spoke out of turn."

Brock moved closer to the desk. "Is the Pike kid a suspect or not?" he asked flatly. "Just answer me that."

"Mr. Brock, I know how you must feel. But you've got to stand back and let the law work," said Turner patiently. "I know sometimes it looks like we're standing still, sitting on our hands —"

"You must have some cause to suspect him. The deputy tells me that Pike fooled around with the other two murdered girls too, besides my daughter. I'm not much of a believer

91

in coincidence, Sheriff."

"Nor am I, Mr. Brock. And I'm really not at liberty to discuss this with you. Go home and get some rest. You're beat. Your daughter's funeral is tomorrow and your wife needs you."

Brock's eyes were hard. He looked first at the deputy, and then back at the sheriff. He opened his mouth to speak, and then closed it again. He shrugged his shoulders in a gesture of futility and walked to the door.

"That's right," said Turner in a more comforting tone. "You go on home and help your missus. Let me worry about finding your daughter's killer."

With the open door in his hand, Brock turned. "If I was you, I wouldn't waste any more time," he said. He nodded his head sternly. "I mean it, Sheriff."

When the door closed, Lockwood said, "Whew. Boy, was he hot." He smiled at the sheriff hopefully.

"He ain't half as hot as I am," replied Turner. "And, Deputy, we're going to have us a talk about that right now."

CHAPTER 8

At midnight the snow stopped. When day broke on Tuesday, the day of Annie Brock's funeral, six inches of snow covered the ground. It was cold.

The funeral service was to be held at the First Congregational Church, and interment to follow in the Green Valley cemetery.

Christie, dressed in her long gray dress and matching bonnet, warm wool coat close about her, drove the phaeton with Gabe beside her on the seat. Vinnie had elected to stay home. Cold, she said, was an old woman's worst enemy. She would tend the home fires.

Christie parked the carriage among the other buggies and, securing Gabe by the elbow, assisted the old man across the snow and into the old, whitewashed clapboard church.

It was far from comfortable inside. The large potbelly stove in the back of the church labored in vain against the chill air that seeped in through the thin walls and rough plank floor.

"Now you see why I don't go to church,"

whispered Gabe to Christie. "It'll take me half the night with my feet in a dishpan of hot water to work this chill out of my bones. Rich as them damn Congregationalists is, you'd think they could come up with money to build a decent church building. Hell, look at the new bank they're puttin' in —"

Christie gave him a silencing elbow in the side. He closed his mouth, but glowered, eyes straight ahead.

Christie watched as several of her friends solemnly entered and walked down the center aisle of the sanctuary. Jennifer Welch and her mother and father; Steven Tabor, alone; Theresa Parr, Catherine Howard, many others Christie knew only slightly.

When Joey Pike entered with his parents, the solemnity of the scene took on a new, sharp edge. Heads turned, eyes were averted, a hush even more intense than before settled over the mourners.

The casket with Annie Brock's body rested upon a bier at the front of the sanctuary, just below the pulpit. A wreath of pine bows plaited with ribbon and silk flowers had been placed upon the closed coffin lid.

Howard and Louise Brock sat in the first row of pews, six feet from where the body of their daughter lay.

At precisely one o'clock the young minister

somberly entered the sanctuary from a side door and moved forward to the pulpit.

After a brief funeral sermon, an attendant stepped forward and raised the lid of the coffin. The mourners filed past the open casket. Annie Brock lay white and lovely in a dress of white lace.

At the cemetery another brief service was held, made the more brief by the bone-aching cold and the rising wind. Dark storm clouds, like an armada of war ships, skudded across the sky.

"Blizzard," Christie heard someone whisper behind her as she stood among those circled at the grave's edge. She watched Annie Brock's casket lowered into the black, cold earth.

In the phaeton, among the dispersing mourners, Christie glanced at Gabe. He had been unusually silent, even for being at a funeral. She noticed with some concern that the old man's lips had turned a pale blue.

"Gabe, do you feel okay?" she asked, fixing the lap blanket more snugly about him.

"Just cold. Be fine when I get home." He winked at her. "Get up to the stove. Maybe a cup of Vinnie's hot chocolate to hand. How does that sound, huh?"

She agreed it sounded fine, and she applied the whip, urging the bay to a fast trot.

After an hour in the warm house, huddled in a blanket in his chair by the stove, Gabe did, in fact, look better. His flesh had returned to its normal ruddy hue, his blue eyes looked perky and bright.

"Just get away from me now and let me be," he warned off Christie and Vinnie. Both had ended up making more of a fuss over Gabe's condition than either had intended. He was not a particularly fun patient to treat.

Christie forced a second hot toddy into his hand, then headed for the stairs leading upstairs to her room.

"All right," she said, feigning indifference, "I'm going. I got better things to do besides nurse you anyway. I can be studying." She came back and planted a kiss on his whiskered cheek. "But you behave yourself."

The old man grunted, but gave her a tiny smile as she walked away.

Because Christie's room was located directly above the front sitting room, with the brick flue passing through its middle, so long as a fire blazed below her room remained fairly comfortable.

She sank down at the small table she used for a desk, grateful, suddenly, for a chance to be by herself. The funeral had taken more out of her than she had expected. And this was strange, for, after all, she had hardly known Annie Brock. She had found it an ordeal to walk past the coffin. For just an instant, as she looked down upon the pale face, rouged and powdered, she saw the dead, pleading eyes staring up at her from under the water's surface.

She shuddered, pushed the thought from her mind, and reached for her copy of the *Iliad*. Miss Houston would want to deal with that tomorrow, that was for sure. Christie's tutor was a short, round, jolly spinster who had channeled her love, which might have gone to a mate and a family, into a worship of the classics and their creators. Each week Christie waded through the heavy volumes, wrestling with ideas and perplexities of men long dead.

At first it seemed a thankless undertaking. When she began her studies, three years earlier, reading had been a laborious and sometimes torturous task. Gradually, as her skills increased, so did her curiosity as to what lay behind the lines on the printed page. Ideas, it occurred to her, did not die, nor did the dreams of man, if they were but written down.

Christie opened the book and began reading, taking notes, underlining entire passages. The room, the storm, the funeral, all slipped away.

When Vinnie called supper, Christie had

finished — had actually gone beyond — the prescribed pages in the *Iliad,* and had begun her study of Egyptian culture for her History of Civilization. At Vinnie's beckon she closed the book, rubbed her eyes for a moment, then got up from her desk and went downstairs.

Gabe was asleep by the fire, wrapped in his blanket. His lips moved in a restless dream. With the effects of the whiskey faded from his system, his color had diluted to an ashen gray.

"I think he must have got hisself a chill," Aunt Vinnie said in a whisper. "He works too hard. Lets hisself get run down. And then the first change in the weather he's got no resistance. Happens every time."

In point of fact, in Christie's three years with the Fletchers, this was the first occasion she had witnessed Gabe being slowed up by anything, least of all a change in the weather.

"I don't like the way he looks," she said pointedly. "Maybe I should go for Dr. Valbourg."

"Poo. He'll be all right." But there was a furrow added to those already lining Vinnie's brow. "If he ain't looking better in the morning we'll have the doctor look at him."

The clock was chiming four in the morning when Vinnie came to Christie's room. The old woman held the lamp above the girl's bed.

Christie was awake immediately.

"His breathing's awful funny, Christie. Maybe we oughten to wait. Maybe you should go ahead and fetch the doc."

Christie was already pulling on her clothes. From her flannel nightgown she crawled into her woolen long johns, pants, and flannel shirt, for she had glanced at the window and saw the frozen flakes tapping insistently against the glass. The wind moaned softly beneath the eaves and a new, meaner chill crept through the house.

In the barn, she pulled the reluctant bay from the stall and hitched it to the phaeton. The doctor, she knew, had a buggy, but it would be faster and easier using Gabe's rig. If the blizzard made visibility a factor, the bay knew its way around Green Valley and the surrounding countryside in the dark better than a lot of men who had been raised here.

She led the horse and carriage out into the storm and closed the barn door behind. Seated in the carriage, she pulled her wool tam-o'-shanter over her ears, took several turns with her wool scarf about her neck, and started out.

The snow was blown on an almost horizontal plane, and the wind that delivered it, howling fiercely, was like a breath from the coldest reaches of space. Christie's route took her directly into the face of it. In moments her face, fingers, and toes were without feeling. She sank as deeply as she could into Gabe's fleece-lined coat and pushed the bay along at a rapid clip.

As they clattered down the frozen street, Christie counted the dark forms of the buildings they passed. After a frozen eternity she pulled the bay into the lee side of the building that housed the doctor's office. His living quarters comprised two rooms in the rear.

She knocked, beat upon the front door, and shouted, but she could not make herself heard above the storm. Her fears and frustration increasing, she stumbled around to the back of the building and rapped as loud as she could upon the closed storm shutter.

At last a feeble light worked through the cracks in the shutters, and she followed that light as it made its way through the building, back through the office, to the front door.

When the door opened, the wind at her back fairly pushed Christie into the office, into a surprised Valbourg's arms.

"For God's sake! Close the door!" he shouted above the howl of the wind. "I'm freezing!"

"What do you think I've been doing out here?" Christie managed between frozen, unresponsive lips. "You sleep sound, don't you?"

Valbourg stood in the lamplight, bleary-eyed, hair tangled, a ratty-looking quilt robe wrapped around his spindly frame.

"I assume there's a problem," he said, peering at her through her cocoon of wrappings. "Is that you in there, Miss Hinkle?" he asked, a pleasurable smile replacing the frown.

"Gabe is sick."

"When did it start? I saw him at the funeral. He looked all right then."

"It was right after that. He started complaining of being cold."

"There's been a lot of that lately — complaining of the cold." Valbourg gave her a wry grin. "All right. Let me get dressed. I'll be there in half an hour."

"I got the buggy right outside," Christie pressed. "Hurry. I'll drive you."

"I still need to get dressed."

The trip back was better. The cover on the back of the phaeton helped protect them from the force of the storm, and with the wind in their favor progress was swift.

Valbourg insisted on warming his hands at the cherry-red stove in the front room before examining Gabe.

"Number-one complaint I get from my patients is touching them in tender places with cold hands."

"Like in their wallets, you mean?" asked Aunt Vinnie caustically. She was worried. Gabe's condition had not improved. Though she had kept heated flatirons at his feet he still shook like a dried leaf in the wind, like a leaf in the icy wind clawing at the windows right now.

They went into the bedroom where Gabe lay. Valbourg set his bag on the table next to the bed. He pulled back the heavy quilt and, while Christie and Aunt Vinnie hovered near, unbuttoned the top part of Gabe's woolen underwear, exposing a narrow-ribbed chest covered with sparse gray hair. The doctor pulled his stethoscope from the bag, rubbed the bell-shaped end briskly with the palm of his hand, and placed it on Gabe's chest.

He maneuvered the stethoscope in different areas of the chest, listening intently.

At length he removed the earpieces, buttoned the man's top, and replaced the quilt.

"It's his heart," he said, rising from the bedside. "Very erratic beat, like a horse trotting on a lamed foot. Very weak. He needs stimulants to bolster the heart's action. Get hot liquids into him — maybe some tea, hot soup. The like."

"I got the kettle on," said Vinnie, and she started for the door.

"That can wait," said Valbourg. "We need to fix him a bed in by the fire. It's too damn cold in here. Have you got a mattress you can set up in the front room?"

"I'll get mine," said Christie. She hurried up the stairs to her room, rolled up her mattress, bedding and all, and lugged it downstairs to the living room. She had a bit of a problem navigating the turn on the stairs, her long, cumbersome burden refusing to bend in its middle. But eventually she made the front room.

"Just drop it on the floor," ordered Valbourg. "Anywhere close to the fire." When all was ready, he said, "We'll all need to lend a hand to carry him in here."

"No, we won't," said Aunt Vinnie. She started into the bedroom. "I'll fetch him myself. He's just a scrawny little chicken anyhow."

Before Christie and Valbourg could reach the bedroom door, the stalwart old woman had scooped up her husband in her stout arms and had lifted him bodily from the mattress. His arms and legs dangled limp in his red woolen long johns.

"Stand back," she ordered. "Clear the way now — here we come." She moved sideways

103

through the door with Gabe in her arms.

She knelt, and Christie and Valbourg assisted in laying Gabe upon Christie's mattress. When he was covered and settled, Vinnie stood up, red-faced and wheezing.

"What you want to do," instructed Valbourg, "is keep blankets and towels in your warming oven. Keep him covered with warm blankets under the quilt. You get the idea?"

"What the hell am I doin' layin' on the floor?"

The three of them, Valbourg, Christie, and Vinnie, looked down to find the patient raised up on one elbow.

"You hush up and lay back," ordered Vinnie, "before I sit on your chest."

"Goddamn, it's cold in here," Gabe said, his voice shaking. He lay back upon the mattress, arms falling weakly at his sides.

"Don't go to sleep just yet, Gabe," said Valbourg. "I want you to drink a cup of nice hot tea."

"Don't want no tea. Just cold. Gotta get warm. Too damn cold at that gal's funeral."

"The tea will help," coaxed Christie. "It'll warm your old hackles. Can't I fix you a cup?"

The old man hesitated, then nodded. "Small cup," he mumbled.

Christie made for the kitchen. While she was gone, Gabe's head turned slowly, his eyes searching for Valbourg. "What's going on, Doc? One medicine man to another."

Valbourg smiled reassuringly. "Well, Gabe, it seems you're having a little problem with your heart. It's running a little erratic."

Gabe nodded. "Been getting gradually worse. I'm afraid I lost my stride — I can't . . ."

"You're doing fine," Valbourg said sincerely. "We need to get some stimulants in you — hot liquid, tea, coffee, soup. You understand what I'm saying. Physiologically a man isn't all that different from a horse. Wouldn't you say?"

Gabe snickered. "If you say so," he said in a whisper. "See if you can pull ol' Dobbin through, will ya, Doc?" His bluish lips moved in a ghost of a grin.

CHAPTER 9

She came to the surface, gasping, sputtering. Her choked cry sounded weakly above the rushing water. "Help me!"

Christie, knee deep in the icy water, clutched her cold hand.

"Save me," she pleaded, but was pulled under again by the force of the current.

Christie held tight, but the girl's hand turned rubbery in her grip. There was no substance, no structure to cling to any longer. It was a white, slippery mass, slipping away from her.

"Fight!" Christie screamed. "Fight the current! You have to help me! I can't hold you if you don't help!"

Christie jerked suddenly awake. She blinked and looked around, disoriented. It came to her — she had fallen asleep on the horsehair settee in the front room.

Gabe lay on her mattress on the floor, next to the stove. Vinnie sat in her rocking chair, head thrown back, mouth open, snoring raspingly.

Christie yawned, pulled the quilt up to her

neck and started to lie back when she heard the tapping at the front door; she got up and looked through the small etched-glass oval in the door at a dark, muffled head outlined against the daylight beyond.

Her boots were beside the settee. She sat down and pulled them on, then got sluggishly to her feet.

Before she could reach the door, the rapping resumed, louder and more insistent.

"Halloo, the house. Anybody home?"

Christie fumbled with the slide bolt and opened the door. A figure wrapped in many layers of clothing stumbled in, scattering snow across the floor, flooding the room with cold like a razor's edge.

Christie closed the door immediately, rebolted it, and then turned, angry.

Aunt Vinnie was on her feet. Her hair had escaped from its combs and hung in frantic tendrils about her ruddy face.

"What the hell do you mean," exploded Christie, "breaking in here like this? We got us a sick man here!"

"My sincere apologies, mum. I didn't know as to how you could hear me above the storm. That wind still be howlin' like a whole regiment of banshees."

"Conor? Is that you under all that trappin's?" queried Aunt Vinnie.

"Aye, it's me — Conor Larkin," said the figure, unwrapping the heavy woolen scarf wound around his head. Exposed was a very red face with eyes like two burnt coals, surrounded by a mop of white curls. He was known to Christie, for she had accompanied Gabe to the little Irishman's farm on several occasions.

Larkin looked at Gabe lying on the mattress on the floor. "Now, just what would be ailin' our good friend the doctor?" he inquired. "Sure he looks a bit peaked."

"Dr. Valbourg thinks it's his heart." Christie's anger had cooled a bit. "We have to keep him warm." She glanced at the door and her tone was mildly accusing.

"An' here I come chargin' in like hell's own hound, bringin' all of outdoors in with me. I do apologize, mum," he said sincerely, his fine Irish tenor vibrating about the room. "Tell me what I can do to make amends. They don't come no finer than Gabriel Fletcher."

"If you want to make amends," attacked Vinnie, "you can start by lowering your voice."

"Oh yes. Yes indeed. I apologize," said Larkin again. "But as concerned as we all of us are over dear Gabriel, lying there so weak an' helpless, I come this mornin', carryin' a burden of my own. My new heifer, my sweet

Coleen, her time is come, an' she's havin' difficulties that I fear might cause her to relinquish her hold on life itself. It was my sincere hope that Gabriel could come out to the place and lend her a bit of salvation of the kind for which he is so well known."

Gabe had slept through the Irishman's raucous entry. Last night, before Christie had taken to the settee, she and Aunt Vinnie had been relieved to see a healthy pink color gradually return to the old man's flesh, his breathing deepen and fall into a regular, rhythmic pattern. Now he lay in a pose of innocent slumber.

Christie asked, "Mr. Larkin, I take it your heifer is having problems dropping a calf?"

"Aye, as I've just said, mum. It's her first baron, and the little thing seems twisted about. The poor girl strains and frets so, but all to no avail, I swear."

"Christie, why don't you go take a look," suggested Vinnie, in an effort to clear the little Irishman from her living room. "You've helped Gabe pull calves many a time."

"Yes," said Larkin brightly. "I recall you've been to my farm on occasion." He looked regretfully at Gabe, then back at Christie. "What say you, missy?"

The blizzard was over, but the temperature

continued to hover in the thirty-below-zero range. It was a bad time for calving. Christie, in her usual blunt way, commented upon this fact.

"Right you are, miss," Larkin freely admitted. "I'm afeared I was in a bit of a hurry to see the results of our new and superior breeding program. These new heifers be a bit higher quality of Herefords, and my bull, of course he also be top-quality Hereford. I fear our haste — the bull's and mine — may cost me the calf."

"Your haste may cost you the heifer as well," said Christie, not unkindly. "Even if we pull both of them through, weather this cold is hard on stock."

The huge barn door was hung on rollers. Larkin grunted as he pushed it to one side. They passed into the barn's clean-swept alley, and Larkin closed the door behind them.

It was surprisingly warm within. The stalls were filled with straw and the half dozen horses Christie saw eyed her with dull interest and munched placidly on fragrant alfalfa.

Larkin led the way to one of the interior stalls. It was a roomy stall with stanchions — metal racks in which the animals' necks could be secured to render the animal stationary — and tight-fitting sides of two-by-eight boards to keep out drafts.

The heifer lay on her side in straw saturated with blood and birth fluid.

As Larkin and Christie entered the stall, a young man rose to his feet and turned to face them. There was no mistaking his identity; he had to be Larkin's son. He was a duplicate in size and features to the man who stood at Christie's side, except much younger; very close, Christie estimated, to her own age. The young man was coatless, and the sleeves of his flannel shirt were rolled up to his biceps. He wore coveralls, the front of which was drenched with discharge from the heifer.

"It's no good, Pa," he said, exasperation showing on his red, sweat-streaked face. "I can get the chains on, but when I pull she just don't turn loose. I'm afeared I might pull her guts out. The heifer's tryin' herself — strainin' for all she's worth. But it just ain't no good." He seemed to take note of Christie for the first time. "Who's she?" he asked bluntly.

"This here lassie is Christie Hinkle. She's Gabe's assistant. She's been here before. Christie, this lout be my boy, Harry. He's about as smart as he is big."

"I don't remember her bein' here before," said Harry with a trace of surliness.

"Nevertheless," answered his father, "she has come to be of help if she can. Gabe trained her. It is for certain she can do no harm at this time."

The young man gave Christie a challenging look for a moment, then moved reluctantly to one side, allowing Christie to approach the downed animal.

She was a splendid heifer, with glossy red-brown flanks, white stockings, and a broad white face with pain-filled innocent eyes.

Christie knelt at the heifer's back side, well out of reach of slashing hooves.

At that very moment the heifer strained mightily. Christie caught a glimpse of two tiny black hooves protruding slightly. But she also saw something else: a tiny black muzzle fighting, it would seem, for the fresh, cold outside air.

Christie looked up at the young man. "You had your pull chains on the feet, Harry?"

The young man nodded. "We ain't exactly greenhorns here, sis. I guess maybe I might even have pulled a calf or two mor'n you."

She looked down again at the heifer. The tiny hooves and muzzle had disappeared. "Would I be insulting your expertise if I told you there's something blocking the canal?"

"Figured that" came the surly reply. "I been up in there. I can't feel nothin' wrong." Behind Christie's back, Harry nudged his father.

"Care to take a stab at it, *Miss Veterinary Assistant?*"

"Get me a bucket of hot water and some soap. We won't find out anything sitting around talking." She stripped off her coat and began unbuttoning her shirt front.

The young man and his father gaped.

"Get along now, Harry," ordered Christie. "I need that water. I don't plan on parading around in my longjohns all day."

Harry hurried from the barn, muttering as he went. When he returned he had a tin milkpail full of steaming hot water and a bar of heavy, homemade soap. Christie had taken off her flannel shirt. She stood in her woolen underwear, sleeves pushed up to her white shoulders.

"Good boy, Harry," she said with a grin. She plunged her hands into the water and began working up a lather with the crude bar of tallow soap. It was tough going, for soap made in a cauldron over a fire did not lather well. But she persisted, and at length her right arm was covered with slippery suds.

With a glance at the two men, she dropped to her knees behind the heifer and inserted her small right hand into the animal. A moment later, she was in up to her shoulder, head resting on the heifer's sweating flank.

A minute of probing, a concentrated frown

on her face, and then, "Aha," she commented softly. "I thought I counted an extra hoof."

"What do you mean an extra hoof?" asked Harry.

"You sayin' the calf's a freak?" inquired the elder Larkin.

Christie didn't answer. Her mouth was twisted in effort as she strained with the arm thrust inside the cow.

The heifer bellowed in surprise and pain, lashed back with one hind leg.

Where she had positioned herself, the animal's kick had little chance of reaching Christie. However, the sharp cloven hoof took Harry squarely on his right shin.

"Saints be cursed!" he howled. "What in the holy hell are you doin' to her? You tryin' to kill her an' me both?" He hobbled around.

Christie paid no heed. Nor did she when the cow lashed back again. Her efforts inside the animal required exertion of all her strength and concentration.

One more agonizing moment, silence broken only by the heifer's labored breathing and Harry's breathless cursing, and Christie pulled her bloody arm from the animal and got to her knees.

"Give me the chains."

The elder Larkin passed the two short lengths of chain to her. She made a loop through the "O" ring at the end of each chain, slipped both loops over her right thumb, and again reached inside the cow.

She situated the loop of each chain around the two forelegs of the calf, above the tiny hooves, and drew the loops snug.

"All right, Bessie, let's go," she said to the heifer. She braced a knee against the cow's tailbone, bent low — dangerously within range of the right rear leg — and began pulling, slow, steady pressure.

The heifer, as if seizing the opportunity as her last, applied her cooperation to the effort, and began a mighty strain.

A moment of intense effort, then, with almost ridiculous ease, the calf slipped out. It landed with a wet *plop* upon the soiled straw. The heifer bellowed. The calf emitted a weak, questioning bawl.

"I'll be goddamned," said Harry. "Will you look at that? Squirted out like a seed out of a grape, he did."

"Actually, it's a she," corrected Christie.

"I be damned," said Larkin, almost reverently. "A heifer. A new heifer calf. Look at her, Harry. Prime Hereford, born to the Rocking L."

The calf lay in a wet, confused heap, umbilical cord tangled about the spindly legs. Eyes the size of healthy walnuts protruded from a head roughly the size of Christie's two fists put together. The little animal's coat, though saturated with blood and birth fluid, was of the same soft texture and hue as the mother's: cinnamon colored with white swatches on forehead, back, and legs. It was a beautiful calf, and for a moment Christie's chest swelled a bit with a mother's pride.

Despite her show of confidence before the two men, it had been her first time helping a calf through a complicated birth such as this one. She was wise enough, and humble enough, to lay up her success to Gabe's continuing torrent of instruction and to a healthy dose of luck.

"Where's the extra leg you was tellin' us about?" asked Harry.

Christie laughed. "I didn't mean she had an extra leg. When a calf goes into the birth canal, the two front feet are supposed to go in first, the head to follow. For some reason, this little critter was trying to get out all at once. Her right hind leg was wedged in with the two front ones. The hind leg was blocking the canal. Nothing could get past."

"So what did you do?" Harry asked, his resentment of Christie forgotten in the face of genuine awe.

Washing the blood from her arm in the soapy water, Christie looked up. "Well, I reached up in there and twisted the calf around so I could pull the leg out of the way. After that, she squirted right out."

Christie replaced her shirt and crawled gratefully back into her coat. Though warm in the barn compared to the temperature outside, she gave a little shudder of relief as she buttoned up her coat and pulled her wool tam-o'-shanter over her ears.

"Well, you did just fine, missy," said Conor Larkin, giving her a congratulatory pat on the back. "Tell me, do I pay you now?"

"Why don't you wait till Gabe's back on his feet, then you can settle up with him direct."

Harry followed Christie from the stall. He watched her intently, his gaze now far from hostile.

When they reached Larkin's buggy, Harry put a restraining hand on his father's shoulder. "Why don't you go in and get warm, Pa? I'll drive her home."

"Fine idea, my boy. Bones be aching fierce this morning. Need a good soaking by the stove. You two youngsters go 'long. An' thanks again, Miss Christie Hinkle."

CHAPTER 10

By the following Saturday the weather had moderated some — for the last couple of days it had hung around the zero mark, in contrast to the thirty below of the storm and after. The change had driven folks outside to frolic and to experience without serious threat the first snow of the winter season. Thanksgiving was barely three weeks away, and despite the sobering chill of Annie Brock's death clinging still in the dark corners of people's minds, a festive mood was beginning to stir.

Gabe had recovered sufficiently to where his constant complaints about having to sleep on the floor had finally worn Christie and Vinnie down. To gain a little peace they had at last given in and moved him back into the bedroom.

Vinnie spent most of the time in her rocking chair next to Gabe's bed. She chafed at being idle during the day, though she did manage to fill much of it to worthwhile purpose, darning and mending.

Christie, in spite of her own full schedule, had been a great help to Vinnie, keeping house and helping with the cooking. She also took the calls and tended the sick animals in Gabe's place.

For all, it was a taxing schedule, and the three were going to have to live with it for some time. Valbourg had given the strictest orders that Gabe was not to move about much for a few weeks. He also gave strict orders that Gabe was never again to engage in heavy or strenuous work. To a veterinarian working with large, at times unruly animals, the suggestion was ludicrous.

"It's either that or die," Valbourg had answered rather flippantly when Gabe objected. "There's plenty you will still be able to do after you get on your feet. Just do it slower. And sit down and take a rest every so often."

That news had probably lent more to Gabe's cantankerous spirit of the moment than had the illness itself.

When Jennifer and Danny came to visit with Christie, the three talked quietly in the kitchen so they wouldn't disturb Gabe.

"Christie," Jennifer was saying, "where Steve Tabor is concerned — I hate to have to tell you this — but you're being something of a snot."

"He's pushy, and he's in love with himself," Christie countered. "He thinks a girl should be delighted just to be seen with him."

"He used to be that way," admitted Jennifer, "but since he's fallen for you, he's totally changed. Wouldn't you say so, Dan?"

"Hard to say, Jen. Never knew him that well myself."

"Well, I *know* he has," said Jennifer with a reproving look at Danny. "Christie, it would be such fun for the four of us. Think of all we could do together."

"I think we should let Christie pick who she wants to spend time with. I mean," Danny continued, "with this thing going on — the killings — who knows who we might be pushing her onto. I used to think Joey was all right. But they're saying some pretty scary things about him."

"They're not saying those things about Steven," said Jennifer. "No one would ever accuse Steven of anything ugly."

"That ain't the point, Jen," said Danny. "Nobody knows who did it. I don't believe what they're saying about Joey. His dad swears he was home the night the Brock girl was killed."

"Fathers have been known to lie for their offspring," Jennifer argued weakly. Though her personal resentment against Pike was strong, Jennifer herself was having difficulty accepting the rumors running rampant about town.

Christie, too, had heard the gossip and had consistently refused to comment. She purposely buried deep in her mind Sheriff Turner's inferences, however inconclusive they were, regarding Joey Pike's possible involvement in the murders of the young women.

"But the only reason they got for suspicion," Danny labored on, "is that Joey spent time with each of the girls that was killed. Hell — even *I* knew all three of them. Not to say I spent any time with them," he added after a quick glance at Jennifer. "Anyway, it don't sound like very solid ground to be accusing somebody on. Not to me, anyways."

Somewhat guiltily, Christie wished that her friends would leave and get on with their sleigh ride. She wanted to get away from this conversation and return to the safety and oblivion of her books. With all the time she spent helping care for Gabe, those hours remaining to her for study had become precious.

"But I guess for some it's enough." Danny, unprompted, began again. It was uncharacteristic of him to spend so much time on the giving end of a conversation, but his fascination with the killings and Joey Pike was apparent. "I was in to Siler's yesterday. Brock comes in — Annie's father — askin' around whoever saw Joey with his Annie. Then he starts talking about hanging the s.o.b. with a strangle knot. He says the man who did that chore for him would have a friend in Howard Brock for life."

"That's just talk," put in Jennifer. "Better to let the guilty go free than to hang an innocent man. I'm sure that's Sheriff Turner's attitude. Anyway, I don't feel threatened by any of this." She gave Danny a playful poke in the ribs. "Not with the likes of you hanging around."

Danny grinned helplessly, then sobered. He looked pointedly at Jennifer. "I can't be with you all the time. Not yet, anyways."

He said to Christie, "If Gabe's got a six-gun, it might not be a bad idea if you took to packin' it."

Christie laughed shortly. "I'd look silly." But she had a thoughtful look in her eyes.

CHAPTER 11

By Thanksgiving, Gabe, to the casual observer, was nearly restored to health. He had had ample time for recovery: there were fewer veterinary calls; cattle and horses tended to move about less in cold weather and consequently suffered fewer injuries.

Adhering as best he could to Dr. Valbourg's advice, whenever it was necessary to go out, Gabe did so accompanied by Christie. His contribution was advice, directing her efforts from a comfortable, nontaxing distance.

On Thanksgiving Day he appeared at the table, ruddy-cheeked and hungry. And, despite the fact that during his illness his stomach had doubtless shrunk some, he nonetheless made a respectable showing, matching Christie bite for bite.

It was an especially warm and joyous time for Christie. As a child, Hap had done his best to provide a sense of home and belonging for her. But some things were beyond the powers of the wizened old bandit. It was not until Christie came to live with the Fletchers that she had begun to truly understand and appreciate the essence of family life.

The weather had moderated further. A fresh cloud cover, like a downy quilt, seemed to lend a bit of warmth to the frozen slope town. By midafternoon, as Christie, Gabe, and Vinnie were finishing dinner, enjoying their pumpkin and mince pie and coffee, it began to snow — not hard, but in the light, delicate, insistent flakes that reminded Christie of the snowflakes in the glass ball on her study table.

It was an afternoon of comfort and warmth. While Gabe napped in his chair by the stove, Christie helped Vinnie clean up the dishes and put away the leftovers from the feast.

Afterward, she tried to study for a while. But whether it was the comfortable, satisfied feeling resulting from the heavy meal, or just a general satisfaction at being among people she loved on this day, her mind, for once, refused to settle down and face the discipline of her books.

After a spell she gave up and returned downstairs. Vinnie had lighted a lamp, and she sat by the stove, mending.

Gabe was reading a newspaper. He looked up when Christie entered. "Christie, my gal," he said. "What would you take to get an old man a cup of coffee?"

"One hundred dollars," Christie answered. "And that's without the glop you put in it.

You want cream and sugar, we're talkin' maybe a hundred and fifty."

"No bargain prices for the holiday?" Gabe queried with a serious face.

"Those *are* my bargain prices. Take it or leave it." She was already moving toward the kitchen.

She returned with two cups. She handed one to Vinnie and kissed her on the cheek. "No charge to you. That was a wonderful meal. Thank you."

For a while she stood at the window, watching the gentle snow drift down in the early twilight.

"I believe I'll go for a walk," she said suddenly. "It's so beautiful out there."

"You better be thinkin' about exercisin' that hoss of yours one of these days," advised Gabe, looking over the top of his *Denver Post*.

"I was thinking of that myself," answered Christie. "Folly always did have a leaning toward barn sour. She's a lazy bugger. I'll take her up in the mountains tomorrow."

"Oh ho. Here's something." Gabe shook the newspaper and angled it toward more accommodating light from the lamp. "Seems we got something in common with London, England."

"If you're referrin' to their queen," Vinnie commented sourly over her mending, "we rightly got enough folks around Green Valley that *think* they're royalty. That's for sure."

Gabe ignored her. "Someone's been running around killing the prostitutes. Seems it started last day of August. As of November ninth, they's five of them been killed. Slashed and mutilated in the most horrible way, says here." He whistled softly. "Ain't that somethin'?"

Vinnie sniffed. "Just goes to show you Satan's at work the world over. Somebody that would do that to another human being has got the devil in him."

Into Christie's mind jolted an image of the Chambers family. She heard, across the span of four years and hundreds of miles, the tortured screams of Hap Hinkle, her guardian, her foster father, her friend.

She shuddered. "You're right, Aunt Vinnie. Damn them to hell."

Gabe read further. "They call the killer *Jack*," he mused softly. *"Jack the Ripper."* He's become quite a legend, it says."

"Gabe, for pity's sake!" burst out Vinnie.

"Sorry." He looked apologetically at Christie. "At any rate, we got our own *Jack* to worry about."

Christie retreated to the back porch for her coat and heavy boots. She had her hand on the back door when Gabe called to her.

"You be careful out there, gal."

Before she began her walk, Christie stopped by the barn to feed the horses. The paint reached her nose across the stall half-door and nibbled at her sleeve, glad for human contact. Folly's dam, Dulcie, had been that way — preferring the company of humans over that of other horses.

Christie forked hay into the manger, a bucket of oats into each horse's grain box, then spent fifteen minutes brushing the animals.

When she left the barn it was full dark; the snow continued to drift down in tiny particles, whispering in the night like a long, hushed sigh.

She walked briskly, footsteps crunching. She breathed deeply of the frozen air, feeling it cleanse and revitalize her down to her toes. And she was breathtakingly and beautifully alone.

Lights from the sparse houses lined the way. As she passed each house, her eyes were drawn irresistibly to look in the windows — those that were not covered — to see the souls clustered for warmth and security.

She thought of Ben Cooper, alone in Mexican Hat. Jane Porter was no longer there. When Christie was living with her, Jane had said that what she wanted, above all, was a home — a solid home, with a husband and a family. From what Ben had said in his letter, she was on her way to having the things she had not been able to get with Ben.

Christie crossed the wooden bridge over the river and entered the town itself. She moved more slowly now, reaching the shops and storefronts in Green Valley's business district. Coal oil street lamps lighted the building fronts, and she looked in the glass windows of the shops at clothes on display, at the tools and leather goods.

The snow squeaked beneath her boots on the wooden boards of the sidewalk. The tiny crystals of snow fell in the glowing circular aura around each street lamp.

It was a night, she thought, not for fear but for thanksgiving, for loving, and feeling gratitude in one's heart for the beautiful things life offered. Fear belonged in another time, along the cold trail from the Utah flats to Telluride; fear of being starved, beaten, raped.

When Ben Cooper saved her, the fear had melted away like snow on a hot stove. Christie raised her eyes to the night's blackness. "Thank you, Ben," she said in a whisper. "I love you."

She started for home, walking slowly, at

peace with herself and the night. Her mind felt clear and clean. The heavy dinner had been walked off, the melancholy given release. She could go home and study now.

In minutes she reached the wooden bridge, stopped at the heavy beam guardrail, and looked down into the icy stream. The water moved more slowly now, more slowly than when she had found the body of Annie Brock in the river. When the snows on Grand Mesa began to melt in late spring, the water would turn savage again. For now it was a black, chuckling pathway cutting through the white snow.

She moved on. There were houses ahead, Green Valley's sparsely settled residential section where the Fletchers lived.

It seemed to be growing a bit colder, but it still wasn't bad. Her cheeks and nose were cold, and her ungloved fingertips, but the flesh was not numbed, nor was it painful. Inside her boots and thick wool socks her toes were warm.

She had gone perhaps a hundred yards beyond the bridge when she heard footsteps. She looked back and saw the figure standing on the bridge, little more than a blurred outline, near where she had stopped to look down at the water.

Christie turned and walked on, steps

crunching loudly in the dry, frozen snow at the edge of the road. Behind her, faintly, she heard other steps crunch. She stopped abruptly, but the other steps continued. When she looked back again, the figure was continuing toward her, and it was moving faster.

She turned and struck out for home, her hurried steps just short of a trot. Her throat had gone dry and her heart hammered against her ribs.

It's someone like me, she cautioned. Someone just out for a walk. But even as she forced these thoughts upon her uneasy mind, her feet, as though governed by a better common sense, suddenly began jogging. They carried her to the middle of the roadway itself, where the snow was better packed, and the going swifter. And slippery.

Her boots slipped and she fell, striking the hard-packed surface with her elbow. Pain rocketed through her left side. But she was instantly on her feet, ignoring the pain. The footsteps behind her had began to run, boots striking the road in an unhurried but steady pounding rhythm.

Christie made for the edge of the road. The going was slower, but there was less chance of slipping. If she fell once more, the figure would be upon her.

She chanced a quick glance over her shoulder and her stomach gave a lurch. Scarcely twenty feet separated her from the dark and bulky running figure.

"Joey? Is that you?"

Her only answer was her own pulse, pounding in her ears.

Terror seized her, and she ran, unmindful of the treacherous surface. Her mind searched desperately for a means of escape. A weapon? What could she find close to hand?

She thought of screaming, but the nearest house was still too far away. She would be wasting energy and concentration better used in fighting.

To fight — was that her only option? If her pursuer seized her, fighting back would be her only chance.

Her flight led beneath the naked limbs of a large oak standing at the edge of the road. She was aware of running footsteps behind, but they were indistinct, at times in rhythm with her own.

Something caught her foot. She was upended, sent headlong into the snow, scraping the palms of her bare hands, landing heavily upon her stomach, and driving the wind from her.

Dazed, she scrambled to her knees. Her left hand fell on something cold and hard, a dead tree limb, stripped from the oak by the blizzard winds.

Desperately she clutched the branch with both hands and broke it free from its moorings in the frozen ground. In one instinctive motion, she turned, swinging the heavy branch in a low, horizontal arch. The end of the branch reached its zenith at the precise moment of the arrival of her pursuer. She felt through the branch in her hands the jarring sensation of impact.

There was a gasp of surprise and pain as the bulky form sidestepped Christie altogether and stumbled into the snow.

Instantly, Christie was on her feet. The bulky figure, likewise, surged upright.

Christie swung the branch with all her might — a batter going for the home run. There was a sharp crack as wood collided with flesh. The figure's hands flew upright, and he staggered backward, cursing in a savage voice. He turned around, dazed, his back to Christie. She brought the branch down across the unprotected back, driving the figure to his knees.

At the last blow, the limb splintered in her hands. She looked at the piece remaining, and then threw it at the figure with all her might.

It missed its mark, landing some twenty feet beyond. But by then, Christie had taken to her heels, confident that she had at least bought herself enough time to reach the nearest house. Its lights burned a hundred yards up the road.

She ran furiously until she was gasping for wind and a knifelike stitch had attacked her side.

Midway in her flight, she chanced a glance over her shoulder. The figure was gone.

She stopped and scanned carefully her backtrail. In the gloom, scarcely distinguishable in the tangle of light and shadow, she thought she saw something moving, lurching along the road back toward the bridge. She couldn't be sure, actually, that she was seeing anything. Her eyes, like the rest of her, could be victim to the fear hammering through her veins.

Without waiting to debate the issue with herself, she struck out for home, choosing to bypass the house she had been making for.

She ran, careful of any obstacles in her path. Above all, she must not fall. She did not feel safe yet. The figure could appear again, could overtake her, could —

At the steps of the Fletcher house, she stopped. She had to rest, to wait until her breathing returned to normal, until she felt the flame extinguished from her cheeks. Her short, curly blond hair was pasted with sweat to her skull under the woolen tam-o'-shanter.

On each side of the front stoop, Gabe had

planted a jack pine. She huddled in the boughs, making herself small and immobile, sensitive to the slightest sound, the faintest sense of movement in the night about her.

From inside the house she heard Vinnie walk from the front room into the kitchen. The floorboards protested softly at her every step.

When her breathing had returned to normal, Christie left her hiding place and circled the house to the back door. She wanted, if possible, to reach the stairs and her room without being inspected too closely. She wanted first to examine the damage herself.

It did not work out that way. When she opened the back door onto the porch, Vinnie stood waiting, lantern in one hand, ash bucket and shovel in the other.

"Well, miss gadabout, 'bout time —" She held the lantern high. "What in blazes!"

Christie's hand went defensively to her cheek. She brought it down covered with blood.

"By the Lord Harry, girl! What happened?"

Alarm such as Christie had never seen in her before showed now on Vinnie's gray features. She dropped the bucket and set the lantern on the washboard next to a metal washtub. She clasped Christie by the shoulders in an unbelievably strong grasp.

"Speak, child! Are you all right? Gabe! Get out here!"

Christie tried to smile reassuringly. "Calm down, Aunt Vinnie. I just had a little accident. I'm not hurt."

"What? What accident?" she demanded. "Why, look at your hands. They're all bloody."

Gabe stuck his head in the doorway from the kitchen to the porch. "What's all the ruckus?"

"Why, you just take a look yourself!" Vinnie turned on him. "Maybe you can get her to tell what happened."

Christie tried to make her voice reassuring. "Aunt Vinnie, I slipped on the road and fell. That's all. I'm perfectly fine. Now calm down."

Gabe squinted at her in the guttering lantern light. "Say, that *is* a nasty scratch there on your cheek, gal. Better let me clean it up for you."

Christie submitted and allowed herself to be led to the kitchen table, where Gabe applied a dressing to her wounded cheek. She had not the vaguest idea how she had sustained the cut. She must have struck something sharp under the surface of the snow when she fell. That much, at least, of what she had told Aunt Vinnie was true.

She had not told them the truth concerning the attack because she didn't want to upset them, especially Gabe.

Joey — she thought to herself, grimacing as Gabe dabbed antiseptic on the slashes in the palms of her hand — or whatever the hell your name is, you won't catch me napping again. I'll be ready for you next time.

CHAPTER 12

The following morning, Lucius Pike cursed the alarm clock, as was his practice, tossed aside the covers with such force as to expose his wife's legs to the icy chill, and threw his own feet on the cold, flesh-numbing floor. Immune to his wife's grumbling, he dressed, then went downstairs to build up the fires.

When the fire in the kitchen range was going, he put coffee on to perk, then set about mixing a solution of boric acid to treat the brood mare's chest wound.

Gabe Fletcher had been right as rain; the slash on the mare's chest was now but a thin, raw line. It seemed impossible that a wound that ghastly could heal so quickly. Removing the dead flesh — that was the secret, Pike admitted. That's what the boric acid did. Well worth the two bucks he had quibbled over with Fletcher. Course, I'd never admit it to him, he thought with satisfaction. Don't want to give him a big head, but the old man was right.

When the coffee was done, he set the pot on the back of the stove, pulled on his coat, muffler and hat, and went out to feed the stock.

Sometime during the night the snow had stopped. Stars glimmered from a sky like black ice, and a sliver of a moon lay waning in the west.

"Cold," Pike muttered as he crunched across the snow to the barns. "Damn cold."

He carried in one gloved hand the saucepan containing the steaming boric acid solution, in the other a lantern.

As he lifted the latch on the barn door, he listened for the horses inside to nicker in anticipation of being fed. The animals knew his step, they knew the routine, the order in which he would feed them. Without variance Pike arrived at precisely the same time each morning. And the horses always responded to his approach. Until this morning.

As he swung open the door, a horse snorted. Several of the animals stamped and pawed the floors of their stalls.

"What the hell's the problem, girls?" he called to them. "I ain't late. You got no call to be ornery." He chuckled and moved down the alley toward the injured mare's stall. He always began the ritual by tending first to the animal's doctoring, and after that came the feeding.

It was a shadowy obstruction, and it hung

from a beam above the alley. Had Pike not felt something brush against his hat as he passed under, likely he would not have noticed the thing at all.

The hay hoist was his first, half-cognizant identification. But then, if it were the hoist, would not the chains rattle? Besides, whatever had brushed his head had certainly not been the monstrous steel hook at the end of the hoist.

He looked up, holding high the lantern. His heart lurched. He held the lantern higher. The saucepan containing the boric acid solution trembled in his hand, then fell to the clay floor of the alley with a dull, ringing sound.

Pike stared up at the thing hanging. His eyes bulged from their sockets, his mouth worked wordlessly.

Suspended from the beam, rope about his neck, was his son, Joey Pike. The youth's eyes were open, fixed and staring. The swollen tip of his tongue protruded from between blue lips.

Pike staggered backward, mindful of nothing save his son, hanging dead and cold before his eyes.

"Jesus God!" And for the first time in his life, Lucius used the name as a prayer. "Oh, dear Jesus!"

★ ★ ★

"Somebody wanted it to look like a suicide," Miles Turner observed to Valbourg. "But he didn't leave a way for the kid to get up there. No ladder, no stacks of nothing to climb up on. And there's no way anyone's going to convince me that Joey Pike was so intent on killin' himself that he slipped the rope about his own neck and then hauled himself up, pullin' on the other end, and then tied off the rope when he got there."

The doctor leaned his knuckles casually on the table where the body of Joey Pike lay. As usual his eyes loomed moist, seemingly on the verge of tears. But, in very truth, his emotions of the moment lay in the exact opposite direction. He was elated to find himself with a major role in what could turn out to be the zenith crime spree in the history of Green Valley. Another apparent murder, and this time the victim was a male. More intriguing yet, according to what the sheriff had told him just moments ago, Joey Pike had been a prime suspect in the killings of the young women.

"Whew," he said, running a finger along the sharply defined indentation in Joey's neck where the noose had pressed. "That's in there to stay. He'll have to wear a nice high collar to the funeral."

Turner stared at the doctor a moment. "His father said he left the house after supper, and he never saw him again until this morning. Can you make a guess about when he died?"

Valbourg looked down at the face of Joey Pike and shook his head. "As cold as it was last night, there is no way I can with any certainty. The cold, of course, hastened the rigor. Apart from that, I would guess it's been at least six hours since he died."

Turner sat down on a hard-backed chair by the rolltop desk. He leaned forward, elbows on knees, cupped hands supporting his chin. He stared wordlessly at the floor beneath the table on which Joey lay.

"All right," he said. He slowly straightened in the chair. "Joey Pike leaves home after supper. Rides in to the Royal Peacock for a few beers. According to Cisco, the bartender, Joey was there till about ten. He may visit someone else, or he may not. He rides home." Turner paused. "Since his horse was put up in the stall, we can assume he made it home and everything was hunky-dory at that time. Unbeknownst, someone's lurkin' in the barn. Maybe more than one person. They overpower Joey, and string him up. He dies a slow and painful death of strangulation."

Turner looked at Valbourg through eyes that were distant, lost in speculation. "You said there was a bruise and some blood on the back of his head. The killer, or killers, probably pistol-whipped him in order to get him to cooperate for his hanging."

The sheriff stood up and walked once more to the body. "Tell me, Joey Pike," he said to the corpse, "Now that you're dead, can I assume that the killing of these women is going to come to a halt?"

CHAPTER 13

Deputy Lockwood sat nervously in a straight back chair across from Sheriff Turner.

From behind his desk, Turner spoke in a low, constrained voice "Do you know the term 'dereliction of duty'?" he asked.

Lockwood looked down and replied, "No. But it don't sound too good."

"Jasper, you running off at the mouth to Brock was something that a first-year deputy wouldn't do. And now the kid's dead. It wouldn't surprise me at all if your loose tongue didn't put that noose around his neck."

"Now, hold on, Sheriff," Lockwood defended weakly. "You can't hold me responsible for what happened. Besides, you said yourself it looked like the kid hung hisself."

"I said someone tried to make it *look* that way. And they did a piss-poor job to boot."

"It still ain't my fault — no matter which way it happened. Likely he was guilty of killing them girls anyways," he went on lamely. "So what the hell difference does it make now?"

"The *difference*," Turner explained, face

whitening, "is my deputy shot off his face on a matter under investigation. I hope you're right, Deputy. I pray to God that Joey *was* the killer." He picked up a piece of scrap paper from the desk, and Lockwood watched the sheriff's hand shake, as though the paper were being buffeted by a stout breeze. He had never seen Turner this upset.

Turner noticed too, and quickly replaced the paper on the desk. With exaggerated calm, the sheriff said, "Just think about maybe if the kid was innocent. Think about that for a while, Jasper."

It was late Saturday afternoon. Christie and Jennifer Welch marched along Green Valley's main street, pausing now and then to look in windows. Their talk was animated and gay despite the fact that earlier in the afternoon they had attended Joey Pike's funeral.

The town itself was in a state of shock, an altogether too familiar condition of late. Joey Pike, son of Lucius Pike, was dead. Whose child was next? Money and power seemed to offer no protection. There were those who desperately hoped that the suspicions concerning Joey were true, that he had truly been the killer. And that now that he was dead — by his own hand — the nightmare was over. But no one, once familiar with the details, held long to the theory that Joey had killed himself.

The fact that the method was different than that used on the three young women mattered little — Joey was just as dead. And the nights still held their dread, and the shadows still lurked just as menacing.

Christie and Jennifer had shed the gloom, at least momentarily, by responding to the sudden whim of going Christmas shopping. Further, they could look forward to the Christmas party at Jennifer's house, a few weeks away.

The frozen air was crisp and exhilarating. The snow crunched delightfully underfoot. The girls went inside a diner to warm up and took chairs at a corner table near the stove. Surreptitiously, Christie pulled off her high-top dress shoes beneath the table and extended her feet to the coal heater.

"You're shameless," Jennifer whispered. "Somebody will see you."

"If they don't smell me first," Christie whispered back. Both girls giggled and flashed mysterious smiles on customers looking upon them with curious glances and raised brows.

They had mugs of coffee, and when they finished, the chill had fled from their bones. They felt warm and comfortable inside.

"You never did tell me what happened to your face," said Jennifer. "Or your hands."

Christie raised a hand unconsciously to

probe the small neat bandage on her cheek. She looked at her friend in a curious way. "You have to promise not to tell Gabe or Aunt Vinnie."

Jennifer nodded enthusiastically. "You have my solemn promise as the most beautiful woman in Green Valley."

"I told them the truth," Christie began slowly, "when I said I fell and gouged my face in the snow. What I didn't tell was that someone was chasing me."

"Someone was chasing you?" Jennifer's eyes grew large. She was thoughtful for a moment. "Was it Joey?"

Christie shook her head. "It could have been. Whoever it was was bundled up so I really couldn't tell. And it was happening mighty fast."

"What did you do? Did he say anything? How did you get away?"

"I ran, that's what I did. Until I fell. By then he almost had me. So I hit him with an old limb. That blew the fire off his wick, and it gave me enough time to get away."

Jennifer was silent. Her friend's story had shaken her. "It must've been Joey," she said softly. "If what they're saying about him was true. And he must've killed Annie and the others."

Christie exhaled heavily. "I just don't

know." She looked at Jennifer soberly. "I do know one thing. Whoever it was, if he comes at me again, I'll be ready."

Jennifer smiled. "You going to carry that big stick around with you?"

"Better than that." She smiled mysteriously. "Remember I said I was going shopping for something?"

Jennifer happened at that moment to glance across the room. "Isn't that —," she began.

At that moment Deputy Jasper Lockwood looked up, smiled, and waved.

"Oh, Lord," prayed Jennifer, "please don't let him come over here."

As though her prayer were the final prompting needed, Lockwood pushed himself to his feet, cup in hand, and walked over to the girls' table.

"Mind if I join you gals?" He pulled out a chair and sat down before they could frame a response. "I could use some company," he said sorrowfully. "Little down in the dumps."

Neither girl felt compelled to ask as to the cause of the deputy's depression, and so, after an uncomfortable pause, he volunteered it.

"Yeah," he said miserably, staring down into his coffee cup, "I guess I messed up pretty bad. Sheriff's so mad at me he's spittin' nails."

"What did you do, Jasper?" Christie asked.

"Let it slip about the Pike kid — being

147

under suspicion for them killin's. Next thing you know the kid shows up dead, an' the sheriff says it don't look like suicide, like they figured at first."

"Well, who did you tell?" Jennifer asked, interested in spite of herself.

"Well, it was —" Lockwood stopped. "Oh no. I ain't a going to make the same goof up twice. The sheriff'll fire me sure. As it is, he's takin' half my salary for two months. An' he's put me on the night shift by myself until further notice. I don't mind workin' nights, but losin' the money really hurts. I'm just squeakin' by as it is."

"What the heck is there for a deputy to do around town at night?" Christie asked. "Everything's closed up by ten, or earlier."

"Walk the streets. Check doors. That sort of thing. Sheriff don't let the bars stay open all hours anymore, so there ain't no drunks to toss. It's the boredom that gets to a guy."

He looked at Christie and she saw a sudden thought flicker in his eyes. "Say, what would you say to maybe havin' a cup of coffee with a lonely lawman this evenin' — say, about nine-thirty or so? I can arrange to be out in your area about then."

"Well, I . . . ," Christie fumbled.

"Christie's spending the night at my place,"

148

Jennifer said quickly. "We've been planning it for a long time."

Lockwood's grin faded. He looked thoughtfully at Jennifer, then back at Christie, and shrugged. "Oh well. Maybe some other time."

Making a sincere effort to couch her words in kindness, Christie said, "I'm sorry, Jasper. I don't think so."

Lockwood looked bewildered. "What do you mean?"

"I mean," labored Christie, "I just wouldn't feel right about it. I'm sorry."

Lockwood's eyes flashed a look of hurt and anger. Then he grinned. "I guess I understand. I'm kind of a rough old cob. Your other friends — the polished-up ones — might get the wrong idea." He glared at Jennifer before looking at Christie again. "But, hell, I warn't askin' you to marry me — just have a lousy cup of coffee with me."

Christie tried to think of something to say that would sooth the snobbish-sounding rebuff she had unintentionally laid upon the deputy. One of Aunt Vinnie's homilies came to her. *When you break a glass, don't waste time tryin' to patch it back together. It's done for. Go ahead and throw it in the trash.* She closed her mouth and said nothing.

Lockwood forced a chuckle. "Aw, what the hell." He drained his cup, stood up. "You gals have a nice day. An' stay warm."

When the deputy had left, Jennifer remarked, "Well, that could have been better."

Christie took a moment responding. She was busy tugging on her shoes beneath the table. "Let's get out of here," she said.

On the sidewalk again, Jennifer grabbed Christie's arm. She was smiling proudly. "I can't keep it a secret any longer. Danny asked me to marry him. And I said yes." She waited for Christie's shocked reaction.

Christie was only mildly surprised. "That's wonderful, Jen. I'm so happy for you. When? Has the date been set?"

"Christmas Eve. In the afternoon. Danny said it would be a good time because work around the place is at its slowest. Imagine — on Christmas Eve. Oh, won't that be fine, Christie?"

Christie hugged her. "Danny's a wonderful man. I know you'll be very happy."

CHAPTER 14

Partly because she was too tired, but mainly because she simply could not muster the interest, Christie did not study that Saturday evening as she had planned. Instead, she listlessly strolled the floor in her room, threw herself on the bed and tried to rest, then got up and resumed her pacing.

Desperate for something to do, she took the shiny new revolver from her handbag, worked the stiff action, getting herself accustomed to the heft and the feel of the pistol. After a time, she extracted five rounds from the box of ammunition she had purchased and loaded the weapon.

Buying the gun had been an uncharacteristic move for her — for any young woman of the time, and Christie smiled as she recalled the look on Jennifer's face when she'd told her. She had refrained for some reason from mentioning it to Gabe or Aunt Vinnie. Not that they would question her motives, or object; with things as they had been around Green Valley lately, most likely they would approve wholeheartedly. Perhaps. She had paid for it, after all, with her own money, money she had put by from that which Gabe paid her for helping him.

She lay the pistol upon the bed and gazed thoughtfully at it. She had chosen a sleek nickel-plated .38 revolver. The ivory grip had caught her eye, but what really pleased her was the short barrel — barely three inches in length — much shorter than the length of the conventional six-shooter. She determined it would fit comfortably in either her handbag or the wide pocket of her coat.

She did not delude herself as to her proficiency with firearms, but she could, with some honesty, judge her skill as adequate. Hap had taught her the groundwork of shooting, with both rifle and pistol.

Christie changed from her dress into pants, heavy wool shirt, and boots. Before leaving her room, she picked up the revolver, pondered its size a moment, and tucked it behind her belt, pulling the shirt front loose so that its fullness would help cover the weapon.

Gabe and Vinnie were seated in the front room. Christie could hear Vinnie's attempt at conversation with her husband, who was likely ignoring her, trying to read a newspaper.

"I'm going to check on Folly," Christie called, slipping into her heavy coat. The response from the front room was unintelligible.

She smiled and slipped through the back porch and out into the cold night.

In the barn, the paint filly snorted at the flare of the lantern.

Christie hung the lantern on a nail, gathered up her curry combs and brushes, and stepped into the stall.

She worked for a good half hour, brushing briskly the animal's heavy winter coat. It was essentially a repeat of the task she had performed that morning, and since the paint had not been ridden that day, it was an unnecessary effort. But it was something she enjoyed doing, a mechanical thing that somehow gave aid to her thinking processes.

When she had finished she gave the horse a resounding slap on the rump. "There. If that don't suit you, tough."

She took another few moments to wield the manure fork, to render the stall itself clean, then she gathered up the lantern and headed for the door.

It was only a blur, a fleeting shadow that instantly disappeared among the row of small jack pines at the edge of the house. Christie lifted the lantern high and immediately saw the prints. The main path to the house was well-traveled, the snow beaten flat by Gabe's and Christie's many passings. But there was a new set of prints in the unbroken snow, and they ran from the south side of the barn and disappeared among the small pines.

Christie stood still, heart beating fast. Her hand stole under her coat to the handle of the revolver.

It occurred to her to follow the tracks in the snow, but when she started out, her courage faltered. Because she had a gun didn't mean that she was invincible. She stood for a time, undecided.

At length, she readjusted the lantern wick and used its light to backtrack the alien prints around the side of the barn to a long-unused door in the barn wall, nailed shut years before. She found a wide crack in the top panel of the door, and it was through this opening, Christie surmised, that the intruder had watched her as she groomed her horse.

A chill passed over her. He had been close, barely twenty feet from where she had stood in the stall. Likely, he had heard her speaking to the horse. She felt suddenly naked and exposed. What had been his thoughts? What had he been planning? And why had he not attacked? Though the door was nailed shut, he could have crept about and entered by the big double front doors, trapping her in the barn.

Eyes and ears keened to the sounds and the shadowy movements in the dark, she walked swiftly back to the house. At first, she was determined to try following the tracks from where they entered the small pines, but then realized she would surely lose them when they reached the well-trafficked road. Such an effort, she admitted, would be useless.

In her room, she undressed, slipped into her warm flannel nightgown, then sat in the darkness by the window, watching down into the silent, snow-covered night. The row of small pines ran on the south side of the house, directly below her room, black shapes, evenly spaced but erratically shaped against the white blanket of snow.

There was no movement, and no sound. If the stalker watched her room, he was well concealed. She smiled with slight satisfaction. And it was for certain he was cold. The temperature tonight would hit zero degrees and below.

She crawled beneath her heavy quilt, yawned, and stretched as the bed warmed and her body unwound. As she drifted down to sleep, she reached under her pillow one more time for the satisfying comfort in the hard lines of the pistol.

CHAPTER 15

December was coming alive with the spirit of Christmas and the anticipation of good times to come. The inhabitants of Green Valley made a decisive effort to put from their minds the horror of the last few months and the missing faces of four of their young people.

The upcoming wedding of Danny Bradstreet and Jennifer Welch was announced at the Christmas party held at Jennifer's home. The announcement was greeted with applause, well wishes, and back slaps to the prospective groom and hugs for the bride-to-be.

Among those at the party, Christie encountered Steven Tabor, the young man people said was destined to play a big part in the building of the state of Colorado. Green Valley itself would not long hold him, that much was certain. The following August he was to leave for England and studies at Oxford.

Christie had plans of her own. Green Valley was not the final stopping place for her either — but she was still torn between whether to go back to Mexican Hat and Ben Cooper or go ahead with her schooling in Denver.

Christie had refused Steven Tabor's invitation to escort her to Jennifer's party on the pretext that pressing veterinary business with Gabe would likely make her late for the party anyway. In keeping with her story, she had arrived a half hour after the wedding announcement had been made.

Before she could even greet Jennifer, Tabor was at her side with a cup of punch in each hand.

"The ever-tardy Miss Hinkle," he said smoothly, pressing a cup into her hand. "The important thing, however, is that you came. It goes without saying, you are riding with me on the sleigh ride after the party. I've brought my cutter and a buffalo robe —" He stopped. He saw that Christie was regarding him strangely. "What is it?" he asked. "What's wrong?"

"Steven," she said, "I want you to listen very carefully. I don't want to hurt your feelings —"

"Is there someone else?" His face looked as though she had just slapped him. His ears, framed in wavy blond hair, flamed brilliantly. His eyes spoke of inner anguish.

"No!" she insisted sharply. "That is what I'm trying to tell you. There *is* no one. There is not even you! And that is our problem. I resent your pressure. I resent the way you continually force your attention on me."

"Well, I'm sorry," he said defensively. "But if I come on too strong it's because I'm afraid you won't give me a chance at all. Maybe if you could be a little less standoffish, and maybe try to see my good points —"

Christie sighed. "Steven, I can't pretend feelings when there are none there. Why don't you try someone else? I'm sure any girl would be glad to —"

He turned to face her squarely. His jaw bore a heretofore unseen stubborn set. "I'm not interested in other girls. There's something about you that I just can't get out of my mind."

Christie shook her head. "I don't understand. Your whole life is mapped out for you. And it takes you in a totally different direction from me. You're going to England next year. You want me to become excited about someone I know is going to be in a different country a year from now? Steven, be reasonable."

Tabor looked disconsolately at the floor. "Those are my father's plans," he murmured. "If you gave me any hope at all, I would change them in a minute."

"I can't do that!" Christie protested, near anger.

Jennifer burst suddenly into their midst. "There'll be no pairing up this early in the evening," she said gaily. "That's reserved for engaged couples." She took Christie's hand. "Come on. I want to show you the locket my grandmother gave me for the wedding."

Christie gratefully allowed herself to be led away, leaving Steven Tabor standing alone, looking sorrowfully into his cup.

On the stairs that led to her bedroom, Jennifer told Christie, "I could see things getting a bit sticky there. I hope I did the right thing."

"I don't know," Christie moaned. "Now I feel so damned guilty. I told him just the way things are. But look at him, for pete's sake. He looks like a whipped pup."

"Well," said Jennifer with an air of dismissal, "better he suffer now than you suffer later. If that's really the way you feel. Let's look at Grandma's locket. I wasn't kidding about that."

She opened a small silk-covered box on her dresser and pulled out the bauble. It was an exquisite example of the jeweler's art: an ivory cameo on the face of the locket, set against mother-of-pearl, with a circle of small diamonds around its outside edge. Jennifer pressed the hidden clasp and the two halves of the locket sprang apart. Inside was a small wisp of yellow silken hair.

"That's my baby hair," she explained. "Until I was about three, my hair was the color of yours now. Grandma is so sentimental. I guess I come by it naturally."

"It's beautiful." Christie took the locket in her hands to inspect its flawless beauty. She handed the locket back and Jennifer returned it to the jewelry box.

They were interrupted by a sharp rap on the door.

"You girls get yourselves downstairs right now," Jennifer's mother ordered sternly, thrusting her head into the room. "Everybody's in the sleighs, waiting on you."

Jennifer's mother was a small, handsome woman, many years younger than Jennifer's father. She had Jennifer's laughing brown eyes, set in a face wrinkled about the eyes with a continual flow of mirth. When she spoke sharply, as she had just now, it was never to be taken seriously.

Nevertheless, it did provide impetus to hasten the girls downstairs.

Christie had hoped to be able to ride in the same sleigh with Jennifer and Danny, but when she reached the entrance hallway downstairs, she nearly collided with Steven Tabor.

"Would you," he implored her, "consider riding with me. No pressure — I promise. For now we'll just be friends."

She hesitated a moment, shrugged, smiled, and nodded. "Why not? But just friends."

He helped her into her coat. It was while he was struggling into his own that he turned his head just right to the overhead lamp, and she saw the bruise. It was a large, bluish mass extending along his jawline on the left side. It was partly obscured by some kind of powder, or makeup, but his shirt collar had rubbed off some of the powder, leaving much of the bruise exposed.

"What are you looking at?" he asked with an engaging grin.

Christie reached out a tentative finger and touched his chin. He winced and jerked away.

"Ow! Be careful."

"What on earth did you do to yourself?" she asked.

He cradled his jaw protectively and looked flustered. After a moment he laughed lamely. "You promise you won't tell. It embarrasses me every time I even think about it."

"I won't tell," Christie promised.

He pulled her through the open door out onto the wide veranda. Most of the other revelers had left. A few were still loading into the remaining sleighs. The night was filled with jingling bells and merry shouts and laughter.

"In a way you were the cause of it," he said, helping her into the cutter.

She settled into the sleigh and he tucked

the heavy buffalo robe about her legs and over her lap. He then removed the blanket from the sorrel and crawled into the sleigh beside her.

"What do you mean?" she asked.

His face appeared somber in the light from the porch lantern. "Actually," he began, "Dad and I were arguing about my going away to Oxford. I really don't want to go. Because . . . well, because of you. I didn't tell him the reason, but I said I wanted to go to Denver and study there."

He popped the reins on the sorrel and they started off at a fast trot.

Several of the sleighs had glass-enclosed lanterns mounted on them. Tabor's sleigh was thus equipped, but he had neglected to light the lanterns.

They drove swiftly through the icy night, guided down the rode by the sporadic string of bouncing lights from the sleighs far ahead.

"He was more mad than I had ever seen him, Christie. His face was a beet red. I really don't think he meant to strike me. It just got away from him. It happened so fast, and then it was over. We both just stood there, looking at each other."

"You didn't hit him back, did you?"

He turned quickly to look at her. Only their darkened outlines were discernible in the night. "Of course not! I could never hit Dad. After all, he didn't mean it. And we made up right after." He laughed lightly, forced. "It's practically forgotten already."

He reached under the buffalo robe and found her hand. "You promise you won't say anything to anyone?"

His hand, ungloved, was firm and warm. Her own fingers were cold. She had left her gloves somewhere, probably back at Jennifer's.

She allowed him to hold her hand for a moment before withdrawing it. "I won't say anything," she said.

The bruise on Steven Tabor's face was in a coincidental location. It could have been caused by a blow from his father's palm or fist, or it could have been the result of having been struck by a frozen tree branch, wielded by a terrified girl out for a walk on a Thanksgiving night three weeks ago.

CHAPTER 16

The following Monday afternoon, Howard Brock sat at his desk in his office. Before him were scattered company charts showing the strata and formations of the earth beneath and around Green Valley County. Brock's mind, however, was not upon the charts, or the ore samples or the assay reports. He was a man haunted, and the ghost loomed in his eyes like a hungry, leering beast. He held it at bay with a half-filled whiskey glass, held before him like a talisman.

The ghost resting so uneasily on the brow of Howard Brock was that of Joey Pike. With each passing day the specter grew more animated. The young man's pleas of innocence echoed inside Brock's head like the voice of one lost in a mine shaft.

He drank deep of the liquor and felt the flames chase the ghost back into the shadows. These days it was taking more and more of the whiskey for less relief.

Early on, right after Annie's murder, Brock had found to his annoyance that he could not drink all the time; there were still the nights, the sweats, the dreams of Annie, so real she might be asleep in the room; and now the inescapable image of Joey Pike, strangling at the end of the rope, legs churning, cheeks suffused with angry red, eyes bulging, purple tongue waving and lolling about.

The glass shook in Brock's hand, and as gently as he could manage, he set it upon the green blotter on his desk.

His sigh was ragged, more like a sob, as he took up a pen and a sheet of stationery with his company's letterhead across the top. When he was finished writing, he folded the paper in thirds, placed it in a long envelope, and sealed it. Taking up the pen once more, he printed on the envelope: TO BE OPENED BY SHERIFF TURNER ONLY.

He placed the envelope in the center of the green blotter. His hands were firm now when he poured more whiskey into the glass, and he only sloshed a little onto the blotter, making a dark wet spot next to the envelope.

Without wasted motion, Howard Brock drank the whiskey. Then he reached into a desk drawer and pulled out the old dragoon pistol he had hung onto as a keepsake from his years in the war.

He cocked the hammer, inserted the long, cold barrel gently into his mouth, and pulled the trigger.

CHAPTER 17

The wind came from the southwest, warm, gentle, melting snow, sweeping across the slope with a brief, caressing mid-winter resurgence of life and hope.

A sense of sheer exuberance drove Christie to saddle her horse and go pounding up the sodden hillsides, dashing among trees dripping as though in a rainstorm. The paint, itself bored with life in a cramped stall, joined in her exhilaration, and was eager to run. When they arrived at Christie's hiding place, the hidden nook by the stream, the horse was lathered and Christie herself was flushed with the physical pleasure of the ride.

She dismounted and tied the paint to a small pine, where the animal began immediately grazing upon the long evergreen needles.

Christie had brought along a small volume of poetry, a somber collection by a fellow named Whitman. Miss Houston, a poet herself, had urged Christie repeatedly to explore the world of verse, laying upon her a barrage of names: Byron, Tennyson, William Blake, sonnets of Shakespeare. It was a new world to Christie, one in which she moved slowly, with steps timid and careful.

Still, she felt herself draw more and more into that new and finer world of which the poets spoke. Here was escape from the cruelty and death, the black terror that had haunted Green Valley all these months.

Christie pulled the book of poetry from her saddlebag and looked about for a dry place to sit. Her usual spot on the lichen-encrusted boulder was covered with a thin layer of melting snow, but she found beneath the spread limbs of a large blue spruce the dry hump of a root sticking above the rocky soil. It was not the most comfortable seat, but it was by far the driest.

Before opening her book, Christie glanced at the sky. The sun, already too long absent from the slope, was again held prisoner by a vast cover of iron-gray clouds. The warm wind sent them scudding along, piling them up like warships against the great Rockies for the new storm now clearly in the works.

Nevertheless, it was wonderfully warm, and Christie unbuttoned her coat and fanned the front of her shirt to cool the light sweat the ride had effected. Her coat, with the pistol in the pocket, hung heavy on one side. It was a burdensome appendage she had grown used to, and she meant to keep it with her no matter what. But still, sadly, it was a continually grim reminder of the dark threat that lay behind the fanciful world she read about and dreamed about.

She thought it ridiculous the way the town, including the sheriff, had finally accepted the idea that Joey Pike had been the killer. The threads of suspicion seemed, at this point, to have all been neatly tied up. The suicide of Howard Brock, the note he left confessing to the hanging of Joey, had been the final talent on the scale to turn the balance of opinion, even, apparently, in the eyes of Sheriff Turner. That Howard Brock, in his bereaved and insane thirst for justice, could have hung an innocent man, obviously had not occurred to anyone. Or if it did, it was quickly swept aside.

Each day, it appeared, the citizens of Green Valley felt safer, as though each day without another killing was further evidence that the right man *had* been hung, albeit in vigilante justice.

In his note Brock had indicated that he had not acted alone; another man had helped him control the struggling young man while the rope was fitted about his neck and he was hauled upward to his slow, agonizing death by strangulation. But Brock had mentioned no name. Whoever it was would have to come forward on his own and make his own peace.

The thing that most everyone seemed to miss in the note (it had been carried verbatim in the Green Valley *Clarion* and also in the Denver *Post*) was that at the time Brock decided to take his own life, he was obviously having second thoughts as to Joey's guilt. Or so, at least, it seemed that way to Christie. The possibility that he might indeed have hung an innocent man was the key motivation, in her mind anyway, for Brock's decision to kill himself.

True, he did not admit to the error in so many words, but that so many people could miss such a blatant innuendo amazed and puzzled Christie. Was she witnessing a mass lie, a town deluding itself in order to put to rest more quickly an ugly and frightening matter?

She wondered what Ben Cooper would do, were he the law in Green Valley. There was no comparing the two lawmen, Christie concluded. Miles Turner was adequate to his job, and nothing more. Since he was voted into his position by the townspeople, it stood to reason that the thing he had most been looking for was a speedy solution to the dilemma of the unknown killer. As long as there were no more killings, what did it really matter if a vengeful father had gone off half-cocked?

Ben, Christie knew, would have considered

such an occurrence as just another inconvenient twist to the case and would, doubtless, have spurred him to redouble his efforts to find the killer before anyone else was lynched.

Ben would also have told her that sitting by a noisy, rushing stream could be a dangerous practice in itself. One could not adequately hear when someone was approaching from behind.

The sharp nicker of the paint jerked Christie's head around. Her right hand dove into her coat pocket, and a surprised Sheriff Miles Turner found himself looking down the bore of a cocked .38 pistol.

For several heartbeats they both remained frozen as statues, Turner resisting the urge to raise his arms above his head.

Christie was first to find her voice. "Next time you pull a stunt like that, Sheriff, Jasper Lockwood will be in line for a promotion."

He grinned sickly, eyeing the unwavering gun barrel. "You're right, Miss Hinkle. Shooting a fool shouldn't be a crime, but it is. Kindly put your piece away. I mean you no harm."

Christie hesitated a moment longer, then returned the shiny new gun to her pocket while the sheriff located another root nearby and sat down.

"You're running a little heavily armed, ain't

you?" he inquired, his smile still a bit uncertain.

"Conditions around here of late seem to call for it, don't you think?" Christie's right hand remained in the pocket with the pistol, a point that did not escape the sheriff.

"Maybe at one time. But, however backward it might have been accomplished, I think the town is finally safe. Or as safe as it ever was." His laugh was forced. "I just regret I can't take the credit. It would sure help out for the next election."

Christie stared at him. In the beginning she had felt Turner to be a competent lawman. She felt he had shown a brilliant intuitive touch when, searching for Annie Brock, he had asked Christie to take him to the area on the river where young people frequented. His investigations into the two previous murders, while they had not turned up a killer, appeared at the time to have been conducted in a thoroughly professional manner.

Now the man sitting before her, vainly trying to get comfortable on the gnarled and knobby root, seemed to be a complacent, self-serving drone, blindly serving the needs of a blind community.

"Do you really believe that, Sheriff?" she asked, unable to mask her incredulity.

Turner looked at her strangely, his head

cocked to one side. "Sure. Why shouldn't I?"

"Because," Christie answered pointedly, "there never was any actual evidence against Joey. If you'll remember, his father claimed he was home at the time Annie was murdered."

"If *your* son were accused of murder, wouldn't you cover for him?"

"I would *not!*" Christie answered vehemently. "Joey Pike was a spoiled, self-centered child. He might have killed those girls and he might not have. But I don't see how you, as sheriff, can just assume that he was a killer because somebody else, some vigilante, hanged him on that same assumption. What kind of justice are we talking here?"

The sheriff blinked at her outburst. "It wasn't all assumption. Joey knew the three girls — at least two, shall we say, in the biblical sense — and had spent a lot of time with each one. He had spent all day with Annie Brock just before she was killed. Now, granted, that ain't hard and fast evidence, but it's also asking a hell of a lot of coincidence, ain't it?"

Christie fell silent. She had a feeling discussion was useless. If the sheriff's mind were to be changed, it would take something stronger than her argument — something, perhaps, like another killing. That thought prompted her to make a last comment.

"I hope you're right, Sheriff Turner. I hope Joey was the one who killed those girls. Because if the killer wasn't him, this town could be in for another surprise."

Turner looked past her at the rushing stream. His jaws were set. "Well," he said tightly, "I guess that'll be my worry."

"Yours and that of the next girl who is attacked." Christie got to her feet. When she reached the paint, she turned suddenly. "Speaking of coincidences, Sheriff, how is it you happened to stumble onto my little hideout? You don't ordinarily patrol this high, do you?"

"I go where I've a mind to, Miss Hinkle," Turner said, getting up from the uncomfortable root. He brushed past her and in a moment had disappeared among the pines.

Christie stood looking thoughtfully after him. She had succeeded in touching a sore spot with Turner, although that had not been her intention.

The question of what the sheriff had been up to piqued her curiosity. As he seldom left town, there must have been something to draw him up the slopes. Her question regarding his appearance could have had a simple explanation, and yet he seemed disinclined to talk about it.

She thrust the volume of poetry back into

her saddlebag and mounted the paint. The horse had managed to strip all the needles from the tree within reach and was now also ready to leave.

The way down the slope was treacherous, much worse than when she had come up. At one point the paint slipped and sat down abruptly on its haunches, sliding for a few feet like a child on a toboggan. When the animal regained its footing, it seemed inclined on its own to take a more careful and painstaking approach to their descent.

The way was churned snow and mud. And it was not until Christie reached level ground that she was able to make out the distinctive prints of at least two more horses. When she had flung the paint filly up the slope, the melting snow cover had been intact, undisturbed. So both horses had come along after her.

The sheriff's horse would account for one set of prints, as he had obviously followed her up the mountain. That left one set unexplained. Probably of no consequence. Perhaps a trapper on his way to check his traps.

As she sat pondering, the breeze that had earlier been warm and pleasant on her cheek turned cold again. A glance at the sky confirmed her fear that the brief respite from the weather was at an end. The clouds were scowling giants, bearing down on the land with black, threatening shoulders.

Despite her chill, something still nagged at her. Was Turner, for all his protesting, himself unconvinced that the killer was accounted for? Why else had he been off trailing through the hills and trees. Had he been following, perhaps, someone who he thought might be the real killer? And if so, what had become of the person he was following? Or the sheriff himself, for that matter?

What if that individual had been approaching her in her hideaway just as the sheriff had shown up? A chill, not from the icy breeze, fingered her spine. No. The paint would have raised a ruckus, as it did at the sheriff's approach.

At any rate, the tracks indicated there *had* been another person besides the sheriff on the slope with her. It could have been, as she had already determined, a restless, cabin-bound fugitive like herself, lured to the slopes by the change of weather and the need for fresh air and exercise. It could have been one of the few remaining trappers in the area, with a trap line along the stream that ran by Christie's hideout. She supposed there could be several people who might have business on the slopes. And yet her heart and her head — the matter of coincidence, and the odds against someone checking traps at this time of day, and nearly following in her footprints as they did so — told her to hang on to her scepticism. Until it was proven without a doubt to be otherwise, she would assume anyone creeping around in her wake to be a killer.

CHAPTER 18

Four days before Christmas, Christie donned her warmest dress and her long, warm coat, and headed downtown. She still had not finished her Christmas shopping or bought a gift for Jennifer's wedding on Christmas Eve. She purchased an exquisitely crafted tea pot for Jen and Danny.

She had sent a small package to Ben Cooper the week before. Besides her Christmas greetings, she had enclosed a new straight razor with a mother-of-pearl handle and a leather strop. She had also sent him a book she felt he might be interested in, by a Charles Siringo, a cowboy and knock-about Texas ranger who had turned to writing to make a living.

At the Empire hardware store, Christie purchased a new cook pot for Aunt Vinnie. This one, made of heavy-gauge metal, came with a lid that could be locked tightly in place. Vinnie had seen one in the Montgomery Ward catalog and had dropped so many hints around the house that Christie came to the conclusion that to deprive her of the pot would be cruel.

For Gabe, an idea for a gift was long in

coming. She ended up buying him a new briar pipe and some tobacco that smelled like a can full of crushed roses. She dropped the tobacco and pipe into her purse with an air of defeat. She was simply unable to think of anything else to get him.

After the shopping was out of the way, Christie decided to go to Jennifer's before returning home.

When Christie arrived, Jennifer's mother indicated she was in her bedroom.

"She's tried on that dress a hundred times," Jennifer's mother told Christie. "If she's not careful, she'll have it worn out before the wedding. Run upstairs and see if you can't calm her a bit, will you, dear?"

Christie found Jennifer sitting on her bed amid a tangle of clothes and boxes. Her expression was haunted by a look of fear and confusion.

"I've lost it, Christie," she said plaintively. "I lost Grandma's locket."

"You lost the locket your grandmother gave you?" Christie looked about at the tossed contents of the room. "Oh, it has to be here somewhere."

"I've looked everywhere." Jennifer's voice was weak. She sounded hopelessly lost. "I always kept it in my jewelry box. Remember, that's where I had it when I showed it to you."

"When was the last time you saw it?" asked Christie.

"Yesterday afternoon," Jennifer answered promptly. "I'm positive. I had it downstairs. Danny and I were discussing having our pictures taken so we could put one in each half of the locket. After that I put it right back in the box. I know I did."

Christie sat down on the bed beside her. "Well, don't worry. It's bound to turn up."

They searched the room, painstakingly lifted every object, checked drawers, looked beneath the bed. They went through the closet, feeling in the pockets of Jennifer's clothes.

When they finished, Jennifer threw herself on the bed. "I told you it wasn't here. Someone stole it."

Christie walked over to the window, pushed aside the curtain, and stood looking down upon the clean, fresh snow. There was a climbing rose trellis outside Jennifer's bedroom window. The latticework was made of sturdy one-by-fours and it reached from the ground below her window to just short of the eaves. The rose vines clinging to the trellis were brown and bare. A few of the smaller vines were black from frost.

Christie looked at the trellis more closely. The top of each crosspiece showed a section where the snow had been brushed off, as though a hand or foot had been placed there. She looked at the window catch. It was unlocked. She reached out and turned the small crescent-shaped cup of the window lock, slipping it into the locking bracket on the opposite sash.

"Who all knew you had the locket?" she asked, turning away from the window.

Jennifer shook her head. "Just about everybody, I suppose. I showed it off every chance I got. I wore it at the party, after you left."

She bowed her head and the gathered tears coursed down her cheeks. "Oh, I feel just terrible, Christie. How can I tell Grandma? She'll be expecting me to wear the locket to the wedding."

With no words to comfort her friend, Christie sat down on the bed next to her and put an arm about her shoulders. "It'll be all right, Jen," she whispered. "If it was stolen, it wasn't your fault. Your grandmother will understand."

"But who would steal it? Mother and Daddy and you are the only ones who have been in the room since yesterday. You wouldn't take it. I trust you like you were my sister."

Christie gave Jennifer's shoulders a squeeze.

She took her by the hand and led her to the window.

"See." She pointed to the trellis. "The snow has been knocked off of each crosspiece, like somebody used it for a ladder."

Jennifer looked at Christie with horrified eyes. "Someone climbed up and entered my room? But how? The window's locked."

"It wasn't. I just locked it," said Christie. "And you'd better *keep* it locked."

"Someone was in my room?" Jennifer repeated dully. She stared at the trellis and at the locked window. "Maybe even while I was asleep."

"I doubt anyone could get that window open, dig around until he found the locket, and then get back out without waking you up. More than likely it happened while you were out."

A thought occurred to her. "Check your jewelry box again. Maybe there's something else missing."

Jennifer dug through the baubles, rings, and necklaces piled loosely in the green felt-lined box.

Jennifer dropped a handful of jewelry indifferently back into the box and shook her head. "It's all here — I think. Only the locket is missing."

"Whoever the thief was had no interest in

just taking things of value," observed Christie. "You must have several pieces there worth as much as the locket."

"Yes," Jennifer agreed miserably. "But the locket was special — they must've known that." She was silent for a moment. "But *why*," she continued, "would they want it? They couldn't wear it, or show it to anyone. Whoever took it has to be somebody I showed it to at the party. And they would know that most everyone would recognize it."

"Maybe somebody wanted a keepsake," said Christie.

They both fell silent at that.

"Something to remember me by?" Jennifer asked softly.

Christie started for the door. "Come on. We're going to tell your parents. And then we're going to tell the sheriff."

They rode to the sheriff's office in Mr. Welch's sleek cutter. They found Sheriff Turner reading a newspaper with his boots off and his stocking feet resting on a chair before the cherry-red stove.

He looked up as they entered. "Huh," he grunted. "If you're out caroling, you're going to have to sing louder. I didn't hear a peep."

No one responded to this attempt at humor. He removed his feet from the chair and looked inquiringly first at Mr. Welch and then at the girls.

"Sheriff," began Welch, "we've had a burglary. Miss Hinkle was the first to notice evidence of the break-in. It looks like someone crawled up the trellis and into Jennifer's bedroom. The room was unoccupied at the time," he added. "Thank God."

"Indeed," said Turner. "So, what's missing?"

"A locket," said Jennifer. "The locket my grandmother gave me for a wedding present."

"Oh, that *is* too bad. Wedding's real close, ain't it?"

"Christmas Eve," said Welch. "Sheriff, can you find the thief and get the locket back in time for the wedding?"

"Well, sure thing, Mr. Welch. I don't see why I couldn't do that. After all, that gives me what — a whole two days? Now if you could just give me a hint as to where I should start looking."

"It's not for me to tell you how to do your job," said Welch, just as caustically. "But maybe if you came out to the house — maybe looked around the grounds — you might find a footprint or something else that would at least get you started."

Turner nodded. "That was my intention all along. I'll be out first thing in the morning."

Christie spoke up. "Sheriff, the thing that has me worried most is the fact that the same person who stole Jen's locket could have just as easily taken her life."

Turner appeared thoughtful. "I believe — I hope those days are behind us, Miss Hinkle. What with Joey —"

"Sheriff Turner," said Christie, "I know that a lot of people want to believe that Joey Pike was the killer, but I wonder if maybe a lot of people aren't fooling themselves."

Turner looked at her blankly. There was a weighty silence in the room as they all waited for the sheriff to answer.

Finally, his eyes dropped and he cleared his throat. "I can appreciate that fact, Miss Hinkle," he said mildly. "I could station a deputy in her bedroom, but I'm sure you can see how that might be a bit awkward. Or I can put a man outside the house every night. Of course, he might just freeze to death."

"The point is, Sheriff," said Welch, plainly exasperated, "what *can* you do to protect my daughter? You may not know it, but it's getting to be fairly common knowledge on the streets that Howard Brock hung the wrong man. Since Pike's death, Miss Hinkle herself was attacked."

Turner looked up. "I didn't hear nothing about that."

184

"Instead of telling you," said Jennifer, a sharp edge in her tone, "Christie went out and bought a gun." She looked suddenly at her father. "Maybe that's what I should do, Daddy."

"Now, as far as you young gals carrying guns," Turner said, "I'm dead set against that. Most women are not accustomed to using firearms. They don't understand a gun's full potential for inflicting harm. In the end, the guns could do just as much harm to our girls as to the killer."

"Balderdash," said Welch. "I don't know how Gabe and Vinnie Fletcher feel about Christie carrying a gun, but if Jennifer ever has to face anybody bent on doing her harm, I would rather she did it with a gun in her hand than without."

Turner gave a weak smile. "So you're saying the sheriff can't protect you. It's up to yourselves now, huh?"

Christie's voice was firm, her blue eyes unflinching. "No one wants to hurt your feelings, Sheriff. But if it's a choice between your pride and me getting killed, your pride's in deep trouble. I intend to do whatever I have to do to stay alive. If that means carrying a gun around, then that's what I'll do.

"About four years ago, some other bad men almost done me in. Someone tried again

Thanksgiving night. If he makes one more move at me, it'll be his last."

In the cutter, Mr. Welch said to Christie, "Why don't you spend the next couple of nights at our house? It's Jennifer's last two days of freedom, so you might as well enjoy the time together while you can."

"After the way you spoke up to the sheriff, Christie," said Jennifer with a short laugh, "I think Daddy wants you to protect me."

Mr. Welch chuckled. "Actually, I do think both you girls will be safe if you stick together."

CHAPTER 19

The nights had a way of getting into his guts, twisting and wrenching his insides about like a big old snake stuffed in a peach basket. He could see the faces, always so clear: eyes filled with trust — and maybe a little respect. And then the look shifting to one of stark terror.

The light died in the same way each time, fading from the center of the eyes in the same way. With the Brock girl, he had been able to stretch the passing of the light for nearly an hour; he had choked her slowly into unconsciousness, revived her, then choked her again. He had repeated the process thirteen times, until his hands and arms shook with fatigue and excitement.

At the end, he must have lost his touch, he considered, because of that tremendous drain upon his own strength. He kept his hands about her throat a bit too long, for after the fourteenth time she did not revive. He smiled sadly at the thought. But she was a scrapper.

If he could find one more like her. The Hinkle girl. Ideally, that would be his next choice, but it was too dangerous.

He gave a dry chuckle and rubbed the tender area above his broken collarbone. *And that gal can swing a mean club, too.*

He laughed outright at the thought, and the sound startled him in the still office.

"Yes, Miss Christie," he murmured, reaching beneath his shirt collar to massage the bruised shoulder, "I think I just might have to settle for second best."

He opened the desk drawer and reached far back, fumbled beneath a stack of old, forgotten papers. He pulled forth an object wrapped neatly in a blue bandanna. He carefully unfolded it and disclosed a diamond encrusted locket.

Stealing the locket had been such a simple thing. He had actually climbed the trellis planning to steal her life, but the house had been empty. He had expected to find Jennifer alone because he had noticed her mother and father at the Blue Swan diner, taking in that fool magician's act. The idiot had been performing at the diner for weeks now, two and three times a week, and still folks weren't tired of his fakery.

Not finding Jennifer at home had angered him. Being deprived, temporarily, of his due, he had felt at the very least entitled to some little trinket, a little souvenir of some kind.

He had rummaged through all the junk in her jewelry box, until he saw the locket among all those trinkets and baubles.

Now he held the locket to his cheek and rubbed it back and forth, savoring its cold richness.

CHAPTER 20

On Christmas Eve the wedding began promptly at three o'clock. By three-thirty it was over. It was a simple, beautiful ceremony, followed by a lavish reception in the church basement.

Christie, as maid of honor, was dressed in positively the finest dress she had ever worn. Christie did not consider herself a vain person, but so pleased had she been with her overall appearance — inspecting herself in the mirror just before the ceremony — that she had half hoped Jennifer would invite her to have her picture taken. It would be nice, she thought, to send a picture of herself to Ben. It would please him to see how she had grown, had overcome her spindly gawkiness.

Steven Tabor approached her at the reception. "I would very much like to talk to you," he said plaintively.

She hesitated. "All right," she said through clenched teeth.

He led her to the stairs leading from the basement up into the church foyer. From there they walked into the now empty and silent sanctuary.

In the days since the Christmas party at Jennifer's house, Christie's suspicion of Steven Tabor as possibly being the killer had faded, along with the bruise on Tabor's jaw. Likely, she acknowledged, it was as he had said — the result of being struck by his father. Sad, but infinitely better than the alternative suggested by her suspicions.

It was a deplorable thing, she thought, while inspecting with a sidelong glance the faint and yellowed bruise. A father who would strike his son in that manner, regardless of how provoked, was a poor father in her estimation. She felt sudden pity for the young man. He had tried so hard to win her interest, and it suddenly occurred to her that her rejection probably amounted to a hurt every bit as painful as that inflicted upon him by his father.

"Christie," he began sincerely, "I just wanted a chance to say good-bye and to tell you how much I've enjoyed the times we've had together."

Christie's surprise registered on her face. "You're leaving? When did you decide all this?"

"Oh, my father and I have been kicking it around for a few days now. Father has a brother in banking, in London. He wants me to go over after the first of the year and work for a while with my uncle. And next year, go ahead with our plans for Oxford."

She was thoughtful for a moment. "Is that what you want? I thought you had changed your mind about Oxford."

Tabor smiled wistfully. "Well, I did. Sort of. But then, Father sort of changed it back."

"Your father has one hell of a nerve."

"Oh no," he answered quickly. "It's not like he's forcing me to go. We just had a good long talk — very gentlemanly — and he pointed out how much I would be sacrificing over the long haul."

He turned suddenly on the pew and looked into her face. "Actually, I have always wanted to go anyway. It was just the thought of you and me . . ." He chuckled unconvincingly. "But, since there's no chance of that, there's no reason not to go ahead with the original plan."

It occurred to her that his decision was not all that different from the choices she had to make about her own life.

"You're right, Steven," she stated. "There's not a single reason why you shouldn't go. A whole new world is about to open up for you."

She took his hand and squeezed it. "I've got to get back to the reception. Merry Christmas, Steven. Have a good time in London."

Christmas came and went without any problems. Christie was glad the holidays and Jennifer's wedding were behind her, because now she could concentrate more fully upon her studies.

Miss Houston, in evaluating Christie's academic progress, was apparently seized with some last-minute doubts concerning her charge's readiness for the upcoming college entrance examination. The portly tutor felt more preparation was needed. Consequently, Christie found herself fairly swamped in mathematics, history, and modern political thought.

At times she felt close to despair, feeling it was all beyond her. The facts she labored so hard to retain seemed to slip through her mind like sand through a sieve. The more frustrated she became, the harder was the struggle.

She lost weight and engaged in long bouts of sleeplessness. Her cheeks grew pale and hollow, and Aunt Vinnie and Gabe began to worry over her pinched, wan look.

Gabe held up her difficulties to her as a valid reason to put off for another year her plans for college.

It was a time of anguish for Christie. She knew Gabe's argument was based on the fact that he simply did not want her to leave. And while it saddened her deeply that he was having such a difficult time accepting it, she could not turn her back on the goal for which she had labored so long and so hard.

Prompted by a sense of guilt, she spent as much time with the old man as she could, cutting further into her precious study time.

Attending him on his calls not only bolstered Gabe's flagging spirits; actually, he needed her help physically. The old man was growing visibly more frail with the passing months. Though the irregularity in his heart rate had stabilized somewhat, he could no longer perform some of the more arduous tasks of the trade. He had not the strength to fight down a rank horse, or extract by hand an oversize calf from a small heifer. It fell to Christie, on these occasions, to supply the muscle, maneuverability, and pulling power needed.

The toll on her own strength was terrific. One day toward the end of January, she met Jennifer and Danny on the street, and Jennifer said, "My Lord, Christie! What have you done to yourself?"

Christie answered only with a tired smile and promptly changed the subject. "How are you two doing?" she asked. "You both still seem to be on speaking terms."

Danny grinned. "When I can get a word

in edgewise. Jen does most of the talking in this family."

"Sad but true," Jennifer concurred happily. "I do let Danny nod his head once in a while."

They chatted for a few minutes about Christie's activities, then talked for a while about all the work they had done — and all the work that remained to be done — on the little house Danny's father had given them for a home.

"It looked pretty hopeless to begin with," said Jennifer. "But we're gradually getting it squared away. Now it looks merely disastrous. You have to come out for dinner, Christie. Real soon."

It was the following week, late on a Friday afternoon, when the wagon's rear axle broke. Danny and his father, Ben Bradstreet, had been out in a locust grove in the subzero chill, cutting poles to be used for fence posts. When they started back to the main house, wagon loaded to the high mark with the green posts, the weight proved too much for the aged oak axle. They hit a deep rut and the axle snapped like a gunshot.

"Aw hell," complained Danny's father. "Now why did it have to do that just now?"

He crawled from the wagon seat to inspect the damage. After a moment or two he straightened up from under the wagon, red-faced and wheezing.

"It split longways," he announced. "If we get the weight off, I think we can lash it together good enough to make it home. Come on, boy, an' let's get these posts out of here."

They began pulling the posts from the wagon bed and stacking them on the ground while the light rapidly faded.

When they were about midway in their effort, they glanced up to see a rider approaching through the dusk. They eventually recognized the form of Sheriff Miles Turner.

The lawman pulled up, jets of smoke charging from his horse's nostrils. It was cold, and the man looked chilled in the saddle.

"Lookin' for a chance to warm up, Turner?" said Ben Bradstreet. "You can drop and help us unload these posts. We been loadin' and off-loadin' 'em so often the thrill's about gone."

Turner smiled. "Can't do it, boys — much as I'd like to lend a hand. I'm already late for another butt-chewin' from the city council. I guess it's pretty much decided by all that the Pike boy got his neck stretched for nothin'."

He looked at Danny in a friendly manner. "You best be getting yourself home to that little wife of yours, son. It don't do these days

196

to leave the womenfolk alone after dark, it would seem."

Danny, sweating profusely from the effort of the work despite the freezing temperature, shrugged his broad shoulders. "That's just what I was thinking. But we got a busted axle. That's why we're unloadin' the posts."

Turner nodded at the obvious. "Well, I didn't figure you was doin' it for fun. Wish I could stay and help, but them folks make out my paycheck every month." He touched spurs to the horse. "Don't dally 'round too long, hear?"

They watched until the night swallowed him, then went back to work.

"Typical lawman," groused Ben Bradstreet. "Just let someone offer to buy him a beer, I betcha he could find a whole afternoon to kill — just as long as they keep buyin'."

Jennifer reached into the oven and pushed with a finger on the center of the pan of cornbread. It was firm, so she pulled the pan from the oven and set it in the warming oven above the stove.

The fried chicken, likewise, was getting a bit crispy. She would not call it overdone just yet. She looked irritably at the darkened window. If Danny did not show up soon, he would once again be eating his supper out of the warming oven.

The tea kettle sang on the back of the Monarch cookstove, and it reminded her she had been about to fix herself a cup of tea.

Steaming cup in hand, she took a chair in the small front room next to the round coal heater, propped her small feet upon one of its bright brass handles, and awaited the arrival of Danny.

What a delight Danny was, thoughtful, unassuming, never failing to thank her for some kindness, an overcooked dinner, buttons sewn on a shirt off center from the buttonhole. He seemed not to notice her flaws, only the loving hands that performed the tasks.

She sipped her tea, rocked gently by the fire, and thought about her good life. The day would come when Danny would move her to the big house, when Danny himself would own the farm.

Jennifer often envisioned living in the house where Danny's parents now lived. It was a fine place, a fine home, with room for children, and a piano —

She canted her head to one side. A sound had intruded upon her dreaming, a sound faint but not altogether foreign. She looked at the clock above the fireplace. It was half past seven.

After sitting a moment longer, Jennifer returned to the kitchen. She examined the condition of the chicken in the warming oven and found it rapidly drying out. The cornbread was barely salvageable.

A thump — sharp, heavy in force — startled her, and she dropped the pan of cornbread back onto the lid of the warming oven. The sound seemed to come from within the house itself.

She stood motionless by the stove, breathing through her parted lips. "Danny?" she called. Her voice broke, came out trembling. "Is that you, Danny?"

The silence in the small house surrounded by the dark night sucked up her words, and her fear spread like a huge sodden blanket.

"Danny, if you're playing a trick on me, I'm not laughing."

Jennifer heard a different sound, a soft, gentle scraping. Maybe wood pushed across wood. There was no mistaking now, the sound came from within the walls of the house.

She looked about quickly. Her eyes fell upon the old butter churn by the stove. She lifted the lid, extracted the handle of the agitator, and hefted it. It felt much too light. Rather than deter an intruder, it might serve only to anger him.

She heard again the soft scrape.

Across the room was the closed door to her

and Danny's small bedroom. The door was kept closed during the day so that the rest of the house might remain warmer. The last sound, she somehow sensed, had come from behind the bedroom door.

She must move, she told herself. She must either run from the house or take a lamp from the table and enter the bedroom. Shuddering at the prospect, she turned and started for the bedroom door.

CHAPTER 21

It was two hours after dark when Danny drove the crippled wagon into the ranch yard at the main house. In a flurry of haste, he unhitched the team, and then spent another twenty minutes helping his father jack the wagon up and secure it on blocks. First thing in the morning they would tend to the axle. Now, he told his father, he had to get home.

Danny saddled his horse, his stomach gripped in anxious knots. He left the ranch yard at a dead run.

On the agonizingly slow drive in, Sheriff Turner's cautioning words had ridden heavy on his mind. Danny was by nature a placid, even-flowing stream, but now, thinking of something happening to Jennifer, his insides boiled and tore along like a white water rapid.

He slapped his heels to the big Morgan horse and thundered over the frozen, hardpacked snow toward home.

A chiffonier stood to the left of the door as Jennifer entered. She quickly set the lamp upon its high top and, heart racing, turned to face the room. It was empty. She was about to turn to retrieve the lamp when her eyes fell upon the closet door. She took a firm grip on her fears, and moved to the closet door. She turned the knob and yanked the closet door open, stepping quickly back.

Nothing. She smiled, feeling a bit triumphant, just a little proud.

From the far side of the chiffonier, she caught out of the corner of her eye just the slightest movement.

As if in a dream, she felt something seize her throat, something rough, and incredibly strong. An arm encircled her waist. She was lifted from her feet, had a brief sensation of falling, then landed on the floor upon her back.

The man was straddling her, blocking out light, imprisoning her.

He had her by the throat. She raked with her fingernails at the unseen face, and her fingernails snagged on something, cloth or canvas.

Then he struck her, and she almost passed out. She felt a hand groping her breasts, pulling at the folds of her skirt.

Just as she was prepared to dive forever beneath the cold black surface, her throat was released. Her lungs greedily sucked in air, and the awesome terror upon her swam a bit into focus.

"Precious," hissed a voice in her ear.

She felt him place something upon her throat, and though she could not see it, she knew what it was.

She filled her lungs to scream, but he clamped his hand on her throat and locked tight, closing off her air completely.

She felt herself spiraling down. And from high above, somewhere above the flood's surface, she heard Danny call.

"Jennifer!"

The shadowy figure jumped up and fled through the bedroom window. Within seconds she was in Danny's arms, and she could feel his hot breath upon her face.

"Don't die!" he moaned. "Oh, Jen . . ."

"No. You're not staying here." Danny was adamant, his voice uncharacteristically firm. "Not tonight, anyhow. I'm taking you to my folks' place —"

"No, Danny," she pleaded. "I don't want to go there."

"All right. Then I'll take you to your parents' house. I'm getting you someplace safe, and that's that!"

She shook her head miserably. "I don't want to go there either."

He had pulled the quilt from the bed, wrapped it about her, carried her into the front room and laid her on the new divan. He pulled the divan close up to the heating stove. She cradled to her the cup of tea he had fixed for her.

He stood now above her, his heart aching. She looked so small, and so beaten.

"Well, where then?" he asked softly. "You can't stay here tonight, hon."

"I don't know," she mumbled. After a moment she said, "I want to go to Christie's. I'll stay there."

He nodded, relieved a little.

Standing before her, looking down upon his young wife, he wanted to fall on his knees before her, crush her to him and never let her go. With manly resolve, for her sake, he must appear strong, must appear in command, no matter how weak and ineffectual he felt inside.

"All right then," he said. "It's settled. Drink your tea and we'll go. We'll ride double on ol' Carp. He's got his wind back by now. Durn near rode his legs off getting home."

She looked up at him questioningly. "How did you? I mean, did you know . . ."

He shook his head. "A feeling, I guess. Some kind of intuition."

"You were so late. I got scared," she said.

"Scared something had happened."

"We busted an axle," Danny explained. "Had to patch it together just to get home. Sheriff Turner come along while we were offloading the fence posts. If he'd lent a hand, I'd been home a half hour sooner. None of this would've happened."

CHAPTER 22

Christie tried in vain to persuade Danny to stay the night.

"You and Jen can have my room," she urged. "I'll be just fine down here."

"No," he said, starting for the door. "Thank you, Christie, no. I want to be there first light. I got to see how far I can track him. And I got to board up that busted window. And right now I got to get over to the sheriff's."

He kissed Jennifer, nodded to Gabe and Vinnie, and left.

"Have you had supper?" inquired Vinnie gently of the shaken girl. "No, of course you ain't. I'll rustle you up something."

Gabe stood about, confused and helpless looking.

"For pity's sake," said Vinnie. "Go on to bed, Gabe. You're just in the way. Us girls is going to have us a hen party."

Gabe seemed on the point of a reply, but he shrugged, smiled at Christie and Jennifer, and slumped off to bed.

Jennifer picked listlessly at the food Vinnie set before her, and then, without warning, began weeping uncontrollably.

Vinnie, never having dealt with an hysterical girl, was ready to send Christie for Dr. Valbourg.

"She's not injured, Aunt Vinnie," said Christie impatiently. "She just needs a good night's rest. Her folks will be fussing over her enough in the morning."

"Oh, I s'pose you're right," agreed Vinnie. "I guess I'd better figure on walking over in the morning and breaking the news to them. No point in raising 'em tonight. Unless you want, Jennifer?"

Through her sobs, Jennifer's response was unintelligible. In Christie's bedroom, Jennifer calmed somewhat and, responding to Christie's urging, tried to tell her friend the details of the attack.

"I think he had a hood, or a mask," she said in a teary voice. "Maybe a bandanna, or . . . something. Something over his face . . . I believe."

She looked at Christie with stricken eyes. "He was going to kill me. And I know . . . I know he'll be back." She began to weep once more.

Christie let her cry unchecked. When Jennifer's tears had slowed, she asked her gently, "Jen, did he rape you?"

Jennifer shook her head slowly, rubbing her

temples as though her head ached. "No," she said stonily. "If Danny had come five minutes later . . ."

"One thing puzzles me," said Christie, reflecting absently. "It was after dark — the normal time for dinner, when everyone would be home in the house. No one's going to bother you with Danny around, so he had to be sure you were alone. But *how?*"

"I don't know, but thank God the sheriff warned Danny to hurry home. If Danny had been a few minutes later, I'd have been killed."

There was a soft rap on the bedroom door. It opened and Vinnie said, "The sheriff's downstairs, Jennifer. He says he needs to ask you some questions, if you're up to it. Shall I tell him to come back in the morning?"

Jennifer got up slowly from the bed. She still wore the dress she had been wearing during the attack. The skirt had been ripped in two places, one sleeve was torn loose from the shoulder.

"Here, put this on," said Christie. She helped Jennifer into her robe.

Downstairs, Miles Turner waited on the settee in the front room. Christie's mind did a quick replay of the day the sheriff had sat thus, questioning *her*, just prior to her finding Annie Brock's body.

His intuition, Christie reflected, had been sound on that occasion. Had they not gone to that area along the river, likely it would have been spring before anyone found Annie. Maybe that same intuition could turn up the identity of the one who had attacked Jennifer.

Turner rose to his feet as the girls, followed by Vinnie, entered the room.

"Miss Welch — excuse me, Mrs. Bradstreet," he began in deeply apologetic tones. "I hope you'll forgive me. I know the last thing you want to do tonight is answer a bunch of questions. But the truth is, the sooner we get on this thing the better our chances of turning up something."

"That's all right, Sheriff," said Jennifer, seating herself in Gabe's rocker by the stove and pulling Christie's robe close about her.

"Well," said Turner, "Danny already told me what you said earlier — that you didn't see his face, you didn't recognize anything about him. But did he have anything peculiar about him that you remember? Did he have a stink to him, something you might recall from being around somebody before? His shirt. Pants. Would you recognize the clothes?"

Jennifer sat numbly in the chair, shaking her head to each question. Christie, standing next to her, saw silent tears spill down the cheeks of her friend.

"What about his voice, Jennifer?" pressed Turner. "How did it sound? Could you recognize it if you heard it again?"

Jennifer brushed away a tear. "A whisper, kind of —" And then suddenly, in tight fury, "I don't know!"

Turner waited a moment while Christie put an arm about Jennifer's shoulders. Jennifer looked up with a ragged, apologetic smile.

"I'm sorry, Sheriff. I truly am. I really do want to help."

"You're doing fine," said Turner. "We won't press it. I don't want to upset you any more than you already are." He rose to leave. "Do me a favor, though, will you? As tough as it sounds to do, just let the thing play around in your mind a bit. Maybe something will occur to you. Maybe just some little thing that will give us someplace to start."

Jennifer shook her head helplessly. "It was so fast. There was only the one lamp in the room, and he . . . when he was on top of me, I couldn't see his face. He wore something — maybe a bandanna." Her voice grew very soft.

Turner leaned forward to catch her words. "How about size? Was he a big man? Small?"

"He seemed . . . average. And he was very strong. He choked me . . ."

"Sheriff," broke in Vinnie, "I thought you said you were going to let up on her tonight. Can't you see the girl is about ready to cave in? You can finish this up some other time."

"I'm sorry, Miz Fletcher," answered the lawman, a bit impatiently, "but Mrs. Bradstreet is the only woman attacked who has lived to talk about it. I know this is an ugly time, but don't you see, I got to know what she knows. She's the only hope we got of catching him."

Vinnie lapsed into a sullen silence.

The sheriff turned anxiously back to Jennifer. "He said something, didn't he, Jennifer? What was it he said to you?"

Jennifer looked at Christie, and then down at her lap. "He said . . . he . . . called me his 'Precious.' And he was choking me. And he kept trying to put this thing around my neck. Only he couldn't because he only could use one hand." She absently rubbed the deep purple bruises on her throat. Her voice was drifting into a raspy whisper.

"He tried to put something around your neck?" questioned Turner. "You mean like a — rope, a scarf, or something to —"

"No. Not a rope. Not a scarf. It was a —" She looked suddenly up at Christie. "It was the locket. Christie! It was the locket — Grandma's locket!"

"Jennifer —," Christie began, stunned.

The sheriff looked skeptical. "Mrs. Bradstreet — Jennifer — you just said you couldn't see it. How can you be sure it was a locket — the locket that you said was stolen from your room?"

"It *was* the locket, Sheriff! I don't know how I know, I just do," Jennifer replied stubbornly. Her eyes were alight with sudden conviction. "I *know* the man who attacked me is the same one who entered my bedroom and stole that locket. And if you find that locket, Sheriff, whoever has it is the killer!"

For most of the night, Christie wrestled with the feeling — the whispered message in her ear — that she was missing something. She tossed uncomfortably throughout the night on the narrow settee, and when the ship's clock chimed five o'clock, she gave up. Sleep was lost to her. She threw off the blanket, dressed quickly, and went to the kitchen to start breakfast.

Over a cup of coffee at the kitchen table, in the silent, sleeping house, she was able to focus on what had eluded her earlier. What if it was more than instinct that led the sheriff to Annie's body? He *did* know Jenny was home alone. She determined to have a private talk with the sheriff. She had to be very careful and not disclose too much.

And then — later on today, if possible — she would write a letter to Ben to see what he could find out about Turner. After that, it was a matter of waiting. Until she received a reply, she could not be certain if her deductions were truly sound.

But would the killer wait? How long before he struck again? And who would he most likely be after next time, if what she had determined were true? Christie herself?

She glanced through the kitchen window at the gray dawn. It had been a cold, heartless winter, and her heart longed for spring. She could think of nothing finer at the moment than to be upon her horse, and be away, riding in the sunshine.

Miles Turner was still in his shirtsleeves when Christie arrived at his office. He sat at his desk, nursing a cup of coffee. His eyes were red, as though he had not slept.

He looked up and gave her a vague smile. "A pleasant good morning to you, young miss. How is our new Mrs. Bradstreet doing this morning?"

"She'll be just fine," answered Christie. "Danny came and got her before I left home."

Turner nodded. "That's a relief. She's a very lucky young lady." He shook his head.

"Too damn bad she couldn't give us more to go on. The tracks didn't pan out. Led straight back to town. And on the frozen ground it was impossible to get a good print to match anything up to."

"You were out there this morning?" Christie asked.

"Oh, yes indeed. Met young Bradstreet at the house first light. Gave the whole place a thorough going over. All we got now to go on is what Jennifer can tell us, which so far ain't been a hell of a lot."

"Well," said Christie, commiseratingly, "no one can accuse you of not trying. You look like you haven't slept a wink all night."

Turner chuckled. "Nearer fact than fiction." He held up his coffee cup. "Seems like I just about been living on this stuff lately."

Christie took off her coat and sat down in the chair across the desk from him. "Sheriff Turner," she said with her warmest smile, "if you don't mind my saying so, you have all the markings of an exceptional lawman. You go about your business as though you've been at it awhile."

Turner smiled modestly. "Thank you, ma'am. I *have* had my hand in the business for a number of years. I guess it shows, huh? Us worn-out lawmen ain't good for much else."

"I have a friend," said Christie conversationally, "who's a federal marshal in Mexican Hat."

"You don't say so? Maybe I heard of him. I was a deputy sheriff in Cortez. That's down in that general area."

"His name's Ben Cooper. He saved my life once. He rescued me from some outlaws."

"I heard the story." Turner's tired eyes showed genuine interest. "I understand you went through a hell of an ordeal. And you showed a lot of courage."

Christie shrugged. "It wasn't about courage, it was about staying alive. You got to resist the devil where you find him, I suppose."

"True enough. True enough." He got up and took his empty cup to the coffeepot on the stove. "Can I offer you a cup?" he asked.

Christie shook her head. "No. I need to get going. I was just curious as to whether you found out anything yet. I think you can understand my being an interested party here."

"Oh, yes, ma'am. Every attractive lady in Green Valley had better be concerned. And she better be damned careful, too."

Christie moved to the door. "You better get some rest, Sheriff. You look terrible. Your eyes look like two burned holes in a blanket." She gave a friendly little wave and was gone.

Turner stood by the stove, cup in hand,

watching through the window as the young woman strode purposefully down the street.

"Now I wonder what the hell that was all about," he muttered. "She ain't the kind to just drop by and pass the time of day." He walked slowly back to his desk and sat down, his mind fuzzy with fatigue. "She was fishing," he concluded aloud. "But for what?"

He rubbed his eyes and settled back in his chair, laced his fingers behind his head and stared at the ceiling.

"Christie Hinkle. Such a *fine* young lady."

Christie laid aside her pen and reread what she had written.

. . . and so, Ben, I entrust this very delicate matter into your keeping. I know that you lawmen have ways of checking things out — ways not available to us mere mortals.

Whatever information you find, you must send by letter, as I do not believe the telegraph totally safe for this highly delicate subject matter.

If my suspicions are correct, we are in a lot of trouble here. And it is possible we will need the assistance of a federal marshal, not unlike yourself. Ben, this is a life and death matter. Please respond as quickly as you can. As ever, Christie.

CHAPTER 23

The next day Christie planned to seek out Jasper Lockwood. She had determined a visit with the deputy was the next step; his authority was the next in descending order under Turner.

She had wrestled all night with the question of how much of her suspicion regarding Turner she should share with the deputy. And how much he would believe, if anything.

Really, what proof did she have, besides her own personal convictions? The fact that the sheriff was one of three men — Danny and his father being the other two — who knew Jennifer would be alone at the precise time meant little. Her attacker could have chosen his time arbitrarily, perhaps waiting in the barn, hiding out until he felt the time was right.

Turner's guess as to the near location of Annie Brock's body could have been, as she had thought at first, a display of sharp intuitive powers — that ability, itself, a mark of a sage and seasoned lawman. Ben Cooper had displayed the same skill in running down the Chambers gang.

As she pondered, she thrust one hand into her coat pocket for warmth and came across the telegram she had picked up at the Western Union office on her way to the school.

Vinnie had written the dentist in Grand Junction, the one Jennifer's father had recommended to Christie as qualified to extract Vinnie's rapidly failing back teeth.

The telegram was an answer to that letter, and Christie, seeing no reason why she should not read Vinnie's correspondence — turn about was fair play — had opened the telegram and scanned its contents.

Standing in the cold, she reopened it now and read it again. Vinnie's appointment was for the morning of the twentieth of February. That was Thursday, two days away. Dr. Newton advised coming up on the train from Green Valley the night before. He had checked the schedule and it would arrive in Grand Junction about ten P.M. on Wednesday night, provided the tracks were not covered by a slide.

Well, there it was. Gabe would, of course, accompany her. Christie wondered if it might be good for her to go along as well.

She folded the telegram and stuck it back into her pocket, and her mind returned to more immediate matters.

Ultimately, it all hinged on Ben Cooper, and what he was able to find out about Turner during his stay in Cortez, if Turner had actually been a deputy sheriff in that town.

And that was it. Short of catching Turner in the act — in the very course of an attack upon some hapless young female — there was nothing at this time to be done.

The idea came with all the terrifying suddenness of an actual attack. A trap! Set out bait and trap the bastard, like a farmer after a chicken stealing weasel. And then wait. What weasel could declare his innocence with blood and feathers all over his muzzle?

And the next thought was the truly terrifying part. Every trap needs *bait*.

Jasper Lockwood sat behind Turner's desk, paring his nails with a small pocketknife. He looked up as Christie entered and his face assumed an almost comical expression of surprise.

"Why, Miss Hinkle. Sheriff told me you were in to see him. It 'pears you're almost to the point of taking up permanent residence around here." He grinned.

"Where's the sheriff?" Christie asked, brushing aside Lockwood's comment.

"Why, I don't know at the moment. We just had us a minute to talk when I got here.

I suppose he might be out checking on the town. Although I can't see anyone doin' any mischief, cold as it is. Is there something I can do for you, Miss Hinkle? Christie?" The deputy smiled, leering.

"I forgot to tell him something," she said, stalling. A thought flashed across her mind, and with it the inspiration she needed.

"I guess you could call it nervousness — I feel a bit silly." She paused and smiled at the deputy as though embarrassed. "You see, Gabe and Aunt Vinnie are going to be away for two or three days. Aunt Vinnie has an appointment with a dentist in Grand Junction on Thursday. The upshot of it is, I'm going to be alone around the place for a couple of days." She paused significantly. "And I was wondering if —"

"You was wondering if me or the sheriff could ride by an' check on you once in a while. Is that it?" Lockwood looked ecstatic. "Why, that's what we're here for — me an' the sheriff."

Christie was sure that when Lockwood passed on her request to Turner, Turner himself would fix things so that *he* would be the one to do the looking in on her.

"You'll let the sheriff know about —"

"About checking up on you? Oh, sure. You bet." He paused to reflect. It looked to be a rigorous ordeal for the man. "But you know, it might just be a better idea, Christie, if you was to stay with one of your friends while your folks are away. That way there'd be no risk at all. If you see what I mean."

"Well, yes, it would. Except I'm really swamped with studying at the moment, and I really need the time alone. Besides, I rather like being alone now and then. Don't you?"

Lockwood looked at her blankly. "No," he said with certain alarm showing in his eyes. "I *hate* being alone. I'm dang near always alone. An' I hate it. The only person I spend any time with at all is the sheriff, and he rubs mighty thin after a while."

Christie shrugged. "Maybe you ought to start going to church. You could make friends there. There's even a couple of single ladies that attend that are about your age. And they generally show up every week."

Lockwood's cheeks reddened and he looked down at the desktop. "I'm not real comfortable around the womenfolks. They ain't easy to talk to, like you."

Christie smiled kindly. "Give the church a try. After you go a couple of times, you'll feel right at home."

The deputy nodded thoughtfully but said nothing, uncharacteristically at a loss for words.

"Well," said Christie, moving to the door, "I'll leave with that bit of advice. Just don't forget to tell the sheriff about my favor, will you?"

Lockwood rose to his feet and followed her to the door. "I sure will — I mean, I won't. Forget, that is."

Christie found herself a bit touched by his concern. "I'm sure I'll be just fine. I just thought it might be a good idea to have one of our capable lawmen swing by once or twice."

"You count on that, Christie. You can sure count on that."

CHAPTER 24

The seed was planted. It was a veritable certainty, in Christie's mind, at least, that as soon as Jasper Lockwood told the sheriff of Christie's request, Turner would begin drawing up plans for a visit, a deadly, one-time social call. Only this time he would be expected. And, if all went well, there'd be a committee of two waiting for him — Christie *and* Danny Bradstreet.

That was the one part of the plan — and the most critical — that she now needed to arrange. It would have been far wiser, she admitted to herself, to have sought Danny's aid and advice before she even went to see the deputy. But in the flash of her inspiration and the construction of the trap, that little consideration had not occurred to her.

She hoped it was not a fatal error — fatal in the sense of deadly. It was most certainly a detail she must attend to immediately.

The house was empty. Both doors, front and back, were locked.

After trying the back door, Christie walked

around the house to where she had left her paint horse. She passed the boarded-up broken window of Danny's and Jennifer's bedroom, in her heart a growing dread, a suspicion that she might have erred drastically.

She mounted her horse and rode swiftly for the main house where Danny's parents lived. Perhaps Jennifer and Danny were staying there for a while.

Ben Bradstreet, Danny's father, answered her knock at the door.

"Why, Miss Hinkle," he greeted her brightly. "Come right on in. You look like you're froze to the bone."

"I can't stay, Mr. Bradstreet." Christie fought to appear casual. "You wouldn't know where Jennifer and Danny are off to, would you?"

"Benjamin, close that door, will you?" came a sharp command from behind him. "I have a hard enough time —" A little round face on a short, round woman appeared in the open doorway. "Why, hello, Christie. I didn't know anyone was out here." Without giving Christie time to respond, the woman reached out a surprisingly stout hand and pulled her into the house. "It's good to have some company," she said cheerfully. "We ain't seen hide nor hair of anybody since the youngsters left."

"Left?" Christie could not hide her shock. "What do you mean, left? Where have they gone?"

"Why, didn't you know?" answered Mary Bradstreet. "They took the train this morning to Grand Junction. Me and Benjamin decided it would be good for them to get away for a while — beings what Jennifer's been through. We put up the money for the trip, sort of as a little extra wedding present."

"But —," Christie stammered, "nobody told me."

Mrs. Bradstreet smiled and shook her head. "That boy of ours. He said they was going to stop by an' see you on the way to the train. Didn't do it, huh? Well, I ain't surprised. That little wife of his got him jumpin' through hoops sideways." She looked up guiltily at her husband. "But we love her dearly, don't we, Pa," she added quickly.

"I didn't see either one of them." Christie tried to keep from sounding how she felt inside — frantic. "I would have thought Jennifer . . ." Her voice trailed off.

"Well, don't fret," said Mrs. Bradstreet. "They'll be back Sunday. I'm sure they just run out of time or they would've stopped by and seen you. Come on, take them wraps off and we'll have us a nice cup of tea."

Christie shook her head and tried to smile.

"No, thanks, Mrs. Bradstreet. I've got to get home. I've got chores to do. And some studying."

As she rode home through the cold, her mind was barraged with doubt, and an insipid but growing fear. With considerable difficulty, she forced herself to think the situation through.

She could, as Deputy Lockwood had suggested, seek a place to stay among her friends until Gabe and Vinnie returned. She could go back to the sheriff's office and tell either lawman — the result would be the same — that she had decided to play it safe after all. That would solve the immediacy of the situation. But when again would there be such an opportunity to stop the killings? Everything was already in place. Lacking was only Danny.

Was there someone else she could persuade to wait with her at the house? Who could she trust to bring into such a daring, maybe foolhardy — surely foolhardy — plan? Her friends were mostly female.

That left only — Steven Tabor, but he had left for England.

She put her horse away and tossed hay into the feed bunker. While she brushed the animal, she remembered that Jennifer had told Turner that Christie owned a gun the day they had reported the theft of the locket. Surely the knowledge that she was armed would not sway a killer, even though thus far his victims had all been helpless. As a lawman, he would consider himself more than a match for a gun in the hands of an inexperienced young woman.

As she wrestled with the situation, and with her fear, she brushed at Folly's coat with increasing intensity. At length the horse paused in its eating, turned its head around, and gave her a curious look.

She considered confiding in Gabe, but first off, he probably would not believe her. And if he did, he would insist on postponing his trip to Grand Junction with Vinnie. That would ruin what was likely her only chance to force Turner out into the open. Without proof, her suspicions would seem totally ludicrous — and if her accusations were made public, Turner would be warned off and consequently wriggle his way past detection.

As far as anyone knew, Turner was a responsible and respected lawman. Without some kind of confirmation from Ben Cooper on the sheriff's perhaps not so clean past, Turner's image was likely to stay intact.

Therefore, whatever had to be done at this time, she must do alone.

CHAPTER 25

Christie stood on the platform and watched the train bearing Gabe and Aunt Vinnie chug out of sight. Feeling suddenly anxious, she returned to the phaeton and drove slowly homeward.

The sky, though it was only late afternoon, had already turned black. Menacing shadows clung to the doorways, the lee side of trees she passed. A breeze stirred, more like a sigh, and it carried a chill that crept beneath Christie's coat and gripped her thin body. When she reached home she set about pushing the phaeton into the shed where Gabe insisted it be kept. She took her time feeding and watering the horses. Then she made her way up the back steps, feeling her knees weaken and her heartbeat accelerate.

Reason told her that Turner could not possibly be in the house. Not yet. He would have had to arrive before her, while there was still plenty of light for him to be seen by neighbors, or passers-by. He would not be so careless — not this one. She had told Lockwood that Gabe and Vinnie would be gone until Friday, possibly even Saturday. Someone with savvy would likely just ride by the place, maybe even just drop in for a "visit," Just to see the lay of the land, so to speak, see that she was truly alone in the house.

Logic told her the house was empty, but her terrified heart said otherwise.

She pulled her gun from her handbag and held it in her right hand, low against her thigh. She swallowed, producing a dry clicking sound, and placed her hand on the iron door-knob. The moisture on her palm stuck instantly to the frozen metal, but she ignored it and pushed open the door.

From within the back porch dank smells of wet leather, wet woolen wraps, smells so familiar, mingled with stale cooking odors from Aunt Vinnie's kitchen.

She stepped into the dark and removed her coat, scarf, and tam. She hung them on hooks.

She lit the lamp that stood perpetually on the wooden drainboard by the sink and looked about the kitchen.

The coffeepot stood in its accustomed place on the stove. She felt its side and found it still warm. She opened the firebox door, placed a few sticks of apple wood on the coals, adjusted the pot above the anticipated flames, and settled into a chair at the table to wait.

When the coffee was hot, Christie sat at the table, nursing a cup for another fifteen minutes. The .38 lay on the table at the side of her cup.

She considered fixing herself something to eat, but in the end decided she was not yet hungry. She realized she was again putting off facing the rest of the dark house.

She drained the last of her coffee, stood up, and thrust the pistol behind the belt of her skirt.

With the lantern in her left hand, her heart in her throat, she pushed wide the door to the dining room, took a deep breath, and stepped through.

Christie lighted every lamp she could find, until the house was ablaze with light. She tramped from room to room, hand resting on the butt of the .38. And she found nothing. The house shouted back at her with its stillness. Her footfalls echoed hollowly on the hall floor upstairs. She heard her own breathing as she prowled through the closet in her bedroom, as she peered anxiously beyond the lamplight into the darkened corners in Gabe's and Vinnie's bedroom. Except for herself, and whatever ghosts her mind had supplied, the house was empty.

She was returning to the front room when

the clock on the shelf began to strike. It struck six times, and the silence that followed its tolling rang in her ears more riotously than the chimes themselves.

She stared about the empty room, felt the oppressive quiet of the house. She smiled sadly, and then sighed, feeling foolish and embarrassed. What *had* she been thinking? Did she actually believe anyone could fall into a trap so simplistic, so obvious that a schoolboy would detect it? Did she have so little regard for Turner's intelligence?

The answer was so obvious it came like a rap from a schoolteacher's pointer. If Turner was to be taken, it would be by more sophisticated means than she could devise. Her best bet — her only bet, after all — was to quit this creeping around and calmly await the reply of her letter to Ben Cooper. The entire matter hinged, she saw now, upon dredging sufficient questions about Turner's past to warrant an investigation, some shade of suspicion whereby she might persuade Judge Tanner or the city council to probe into the sheriff's movements.

Tomorrow she would seek out a friend in town with whom she could stay until Gabe and Aunt Vinnie's return.

And then, in time, when she had in hand Ben Cooper's response to her letter, she could lay the entire matter before Judge Tanner and let the authorities deal with Turner.

With a peaceful resolve, she got ready for bed.

It could have been a regiment of the long, daggerlike icicles clinging to the eaves, melting free, dropping suddenly, and crashing into a thousand pieces on the crusted snow below. Glass shattering sounded like that.

Christie knew it for what it was. She lay listening, eyes open to the dark, heart hammering against her ribs. She reached for the .38 revolver beneath her pillow and slipped from beneath the covers.

There had been but the one sound. Though the house was pressed in tomblike stillness, she must assume that the intruder had gained entrance.

The faint gray of first dawn showed in her east window, but the house lay still in near darkness. Familiar shapes were but vague outlines in the gloom.

She stepped without sound to the lamp on her dresser top, picked up a match, and was about to strike it when she hesitated. Instead, she dropped the match and reached for a pair of pants lying across a chair. She slipped them on beneath her nightgown and moved to the open door of her bedroom.

A draft of cold night air struck her in the face. She had a momentary impression of a faint scuffing sound from below. A boot heel on the dining-room carpet?

Pressing her back against the wall, she moved down the hallway toward the staircase. In her right hand she gripped the pistol.

She moved slowly, bare feet testing each step before applying her weight, eyes straining against the darkness. The one thing she could not bring under control was her racing heart.

Midway down, the stairs made a turn to the right, and Christie edged her way toward that landing, fighting down with each step paroxysms of fear, fighting back the panic urge to flee back to her room and cower behind its locked door. She forced herself on, down, down, a step at a time.

As she moved, she placed her feet close to the wall, partly because the wall gave support to her quaking knees; further, she knew that the loose steps of the stairs were less apt to creak when weight was applied near the wall and not in the middle of the step.

When she reached the bottom, she stopped. There she stood, against the wall, waiting for several minutes. Reason told her to let Turner make the first move, betray his position. It was critical that she locate him first, and somehow, in the dark, bring him under the muzzle of the .38 before he could get within striking distance of her.

She listened intently, lips parted in concentration. Her skin beneath the flannel gown grew chilled and gooseflesh erupted. Her bare feet ached on the cold floor.

Suddenly, he was there, looming large and dark before her.

She froze. Her arm with the gun felt wooden and lifeless.

He seized her hand, and wrenched the gun from her fingers. The next moment she was clasped fiercely by the arm and slammed into the wall, striking it with stunning force. She rebounded, falling backward against the stairs. She did not lose consciousness, but she was dazed, immobile.

It was the laugh that brought her back. She saw him standing above her, a shadow in a fearsome black form.

Panic seized her. She tried to propel herself up the stairs on her back, pushing with her legs, pushing away from him. Pain rocketed up her right leg and exploded in her hip. She screamed.

"Just like a crippled bird, ain't ya?" he said, and he took a heavy step closer to her.

The voice! It was *not* Turner.

"Yes, ma'am," he said, "I should've been

a vet myself. Many's the crippled bird I treated in my day. Old Doc Lockwood." He laughed. "How does that sound to you, honey? Or would Doc Jasper sound better? Bet you wouldn't mind having that cup of coffee with me then, you and your snooty friends."

She twisted to her side, raising the injured hip and leg. In this position she was able to slide a bit further up the stairs. She inched her way, like a halfcrushed worm.

He followed, a step at a time, stepping to the side of the injured girl. "Christie, darlin', you're laborin' in vain."

She kneed him in the groin with her good leg.

He doubled up for a moment, then lunged at her, his hands around her neck until she passed out.

When she awakened, she could feel him dragging her down the stairs and out into the dining room.

The pain was too intense for her even to cry out. The room swam before her eyes. A red haze, like a curtain of crimson gauze, floated about her, and she was only dimly aware of being dragged.

The world rocked on a sea of agony as Lockwood dropped her unceremoniously onto one of the chairs at the dining room table. He found a lamp and lighted it. In a most casual manner, he pulled out the chair across from her and sat down.

"Cozy, ain't it?" he said.

Christie tried to speak. Her lips moved, but no sound came out.

Lockwood looked at her thoughtfully. "Right nice of you to let me know you'd be alone. Of course, I didn't tell the sheriff — we don't need him to have us some fun."

Fear settled into her like the cold, a gripping force, making her limbs and her mind useless. She was certain now that she was going to die. She tried to think, but her thoughts flowed slowly, like cold honey.

"I bet you think a lot more of Ol' Jasper now, don't you? I'm a trace smarter than I let on."

Christie made an effort to focus her eyes on the man, to listen to what he was saying. She was controlling the pain better now. If only she could distract him, find a way to reach her gun, which he had tucked under his belt. Or his own six-gun holstered beneath his waist.

"Why didn't you kill me back there on the stairs?" she asked, softly.

"I could have, you know," he said musingly.

He looked at her closely. "You have pretty blue eyes," he said abruptly.

Christie shuddered.

Smiling, he got lazily to his feet and rounded the table to her. He reached down and twined the fingers of his left hand in her hair. She cringed, clamping her jaw against the pain. He jerked her head back, pulling her hair so sharply tears came rushing to her eyes.

By her hair, he pulled her upright in the chair; the pain in Christie's hip and leg erupted again, and she screamed.

Holding her head firmly back, he allowed her to sob for a moment, then bent down and kissed her on the lips. Then he grabbed her throat with one hand and began to squeeze with exaggerated slowness.

Christie chose that moment to act. She seized her pistol from Lockwood's belt. She clasped it in her left hand because of the broken right thumb.

"Why, you little bitch!" He stepped back.

"Shut up!" She pulled back the hammer sharply. "Don't move, you bastard!"

Lockwood stared at her a moment, glanced at the gun, then, to Christie's surprise and confusion, smiled.

Keeping the barrel leveled on Lockwood's chest, Christie eased herself around on the chair. The entire right side of her body was on fire. She could not guess to what extent she had been injured, but she knew it was serious. Her leg most surely was broken. She feared she might pass out at any time, and if that happened, all was lost.

He looked at her, an infuriatingly complacent smile on his lips.

He opened his hands in an expansive gesture. "Go ahead and shoot, woman. You got the gun. Though you might want to check first to see whether or not I took the loads out of it. I can't rightly remember."

Christie flinched. She stared at him through exhausted, pain-filled eyes. Had there been enough time for him to empty the gun while she was unconscious on the stairs? In the dark, before he lit the lamp? Was Jasper Lockwood really that smart — or was he bluffing?

"An' now, Christie Hinkle, it's time we . . ."

Christie raised the pistol, shoved the barrel against Lockwood's chest, and pulled the trigger.

Lockwood seized her by the front of her nightshirt and pulled. The material began to tear as he fell to the floor.

CHAPTER 26

"You'll have a limp, but you'll be all right," Doctor Valbourg told her. He had been visiting Christie nearly every day for what seemed like weeks now.

"If you like," he ventured, "I can show you some exercises that should help, to a degree. And I'd be glad to help you do them."

"Ain't no need for that," Vinnie said firmly. "I'll help her with any exercisin' needs doin'."

Valbourg smiled and reached for his coat. "Of course, Mrs. Fletcher. She could not be in better hands."

After Valbourg left, Christie sat with a quilt across her legs, staring out through the window at the ugly world beyond: brown, melting slush; gray naked tree limbs; dismal clouds against a dismal, ashen sky.

Her heart gladdened when she saw Gabe coming down the road in his phaeton. She waited impatiently for him while he put up the carriage and the bay horse.

The only bright spots in the long, dark days of her convalescence had been her reading and the conversations she shared with the old man from his chair by the stove.

She had had considerable time to brood, and to entertain virulent nightmares over her encounter with Green Valley's killer.

As word got about concerning the identification and death of the killer, the town breathed a collective sigh of relief. But a kind of hushed embarrassment accompanied that relief. That the killer had been the town's deputy sheriff — it was almost inconceivable.

Nothing was said openly to him, but Turner, after encountering for a time the silent, speculative glances, and the too-quickly turned heads, one day quietly tendered his resignation and left town.

Ironic, thought Christie, in light of the letter she had received only a few days later from Deputy Marshal Cecil Akins in Mexican Hat, totally vindicating Sheriff Miles Turner and rendering her own suspicions of the man as completely ridiculous. Turner's record as a lawman, throughout the various towns he had served, was immaculate — even admirable, in a few cases.

Christie did think it strange that Ben had delegated to Akins the chore of answering her letter regarding Turner. But then she recalled in his last letter his statement that he was now turning a lot of work over to the deputy.

Gabe's boots clumping across the floor

brought Christie back. The old man appeared before her, ruddy-cheeked and sparkly-eyed from his excursion outdoors. He seemed about to burst with vitality.

"Before you start hollerin' at me — yes, I got every dad-blamed thing on your list, from buttons to pencils to crutches. And the doc says you ain't to start using them crutches until Monday next. You got that?"

He held out a small flat box to her. It was tied with a blue silk ribbon. "I got you a little something besides," he said gruffly. "It ain't much — just a diary. But I thought it might give you something to do besides read and argue with me."

She took the box and inspected it with quiet eyes. "I've never had a diary before. Never even thought about having one." She pulled the ribbon loose, lifted the lid, and took out the small book. Its cover was leather, with a spray of embossed roses on the front and her name in gold letters stamped in a lower corner. "I guess it's high time I gave it a try. Thank you, Gabe. It's beautiful."

He leaned down and kissed her on the cheek. "And you're most welcome."

He sat down in his chair by the stove, pulled off his wet boots, and tossed them carelessly in the corner. He leaned back and sniffed the air, wrinkling his nose.

"Oh, by the bye." Gabe fumbled through his pockets. "Got a couple of letters for you." He pulled two wrinkled envelopes from a hip pocket, padded in his stocking feet over to the settee, and presented them to her. "One is from the college."

Christie took the envelopes. Her hand trembled a bit. The envelope on top bore the stamped logo of the University of Denver. Her heart jumped and she found herself short of breath.

During the first week of her convalescence, Miss Houston, her tutor, hit upon the inspiration of capitalizing upon Christie's new status as a heroine. She had gone about the town collecting signatures and statements from prominent townspeople, extolling Christie's sterling character and initiative. The teacher had submitted, along with this impressive package, a draft of Christie's grades and her own — Miss Houston's — professional opinion of Christie's aptitude as a student.

Christie had found out about her tutor's campaign a few days after the application was sent off. Part of her restlessness at being cooped up had been due to her nerve-racking vigil, awaiting the entrance committee's verdict.

As she was tearing open the envelope, Aunt Vinnie came in from the kitchen. She looked at Christie's pale, anxious face, and then at Gabe.

"What's going on?" she demanded. She spied the letter in Christie's hands. "Oh," she said, sounding uncharacteristically meek.

Christie looked up. "I guess I'm kind of forgetting the order of things around here." She smiled at the old lady. "Open this and read it for me, will you, Aunt Vinnie?"

Vinnie's face flushed. "Why, I —"

"I'd consider it a favor," implored Christie. "I don't think I can do it."

Vinnie took the letter, handling it gingerly by the corners. She carefully eased open the flap and pulled out the single sheet.

The letter was short. The old woman read it in a near monotone.

> Office of the Registrar
> University of Denver
> Denver, Colorado

Dear Miss Hinkle:

It is with great pleasure that we welcome you to the student body for the class beginning August 28, 1889. We feel that your presence will constitute a positive influence on our campus and we look forward to sharing with you this next academic year. Congratulations.

Respectfully,
A. J. Meyerson, Ph.D.
Registrar

"Yahoo!" shouted Gabe. He leaped to his feet and threw his arms about his wife. Together they rushed to the settee and gathered Christie in their arms, unmindful of her tender injuries.

"Gal, you're on your way!" Gabe laughed joyously.

"We're so proud of you, Christie!" Vinnie said, two small tears coursing down either cheek.

Christie could only smile and nod. She found she could not speak past her constricted throat. She had to blink rapidly to fight back tears of joy and relief.

"Well, let's see that other letter," Vinnie said exuberantly. "Way our luck's going today, shoot, it might be a deed to a gold mine."

Christie offered up the letter with a smile.

"Why, it's from Janey," said Vinnie. "Never mind writing to her old aunt and uncle — not when she's got Christie she can correspond with." She said it in a lightly

joking manner as she tore open the envelope.

She glanced up and down the page, focusing
her eyes through her thick glasses.

Her smile wilted, then faded altogether. She
paused, looked up, and coughed.

"Well." She handed the letter back to Christie and said gently, "Honey, I think this one
you best read yourself."

The old woman turned and started for the
kitchen. "Come on, Gabe. I need you to peel
some onions."

Gabe looked after her a moment, a puzzled
expression on his seamed face, then mutely
followed.

Christie, bewilderment in her blue eyes, a
strange, nagging dread in the pit of her stomach, looked at the letter in her hand. She recognized Jane Porter's small, exactingly neat
script.

Dearest Christie,

I hope this letter finds you recovering
nicely from your injuries.

There was a fine article in the Durango
paper, glorifying your brave exploits. On
the very same day as the article appeared,
I received a letter from Aunt Vinnie, giving
all the details of your fight with that terrible
man. How I thank God that you were

spared and that the world is rid of such as he.

Well, Christie, enough on that. I'm sure that is a part of your life you would like soon to forget.

We are doing fine here. John works very hard in the store and we are putting money by. If all goes well, our living expenses will soon be increased due to the addition of one more person. It happens I am with child. John and I could not be more thrilled.

Christie, dear, I have sad news for you. Our friend, Ben Cooper, has passed away.

The paper in Christie's hand began to tremble.

I do not know all the details as yet. I received a letter from Cecil Akins yesterday, and he asked me if I would be the one to inform you of the news. I wanted to come to Green Valley in person, to be there with you, but my doctor advised against the trip.

As I say, the details are a bit sketchy. Mexican Hat had an epidemic of mumps and it seems Ben came down with a severe case. Pneumonia is what finally took him.

But you know he had been in ill health ever since the wound he suffered at the hands of the Utes.

It would be my hope, Christie, that you would bear this sad news as bravely as you have faced all the other trials you have encountered in your young life. Ben's love for you was genuine and touching to behold, and as you grieve for him, you may take some comfort from that fact. I share your loss, and will be grieving with you.

The words flowed together, seen through Christie's blinding tears. She let the letter fall to the floor and buried her face in her hands.

After a while, she was able to reread Jane's letter without crying. Then she read her acceptance letter again and held them both to her heart.